HILLCREST
JOURNAL

HILLCREST JOURNAL

To Hage –
Best wishes!

John Schreiber (signature)

John Schreiber

To order additional copies of this book, contact:
Xlibris Corporation
1-888-795-4274
www.Xlibris.com
Orders@Xlibris.com
16003

I didn't set out to write a book.
It just sort of happened.
Like life.

Chad Wilson

FIRST SEMESTER, FIRST QUARTER

Monday: This is stupid. You're not even going to read it. How can you grade it? I can't write a page a day. I have nothing to write. I have nothing to write. I have nothing to write. There—how's that for filler?

My name is Chad Wilson. My name is Chad Wilson. This is really stupid. But if you never read this, you'll never know how stupid it really is. Stupid.

Chad Wilson. 17. I graduate in June. I'll be 18 in July. I don't know what I'll do after that.

This is stupid, Mrs. Webster, but you want a page a day.

I need the grade.

My father's name is Charles. Mother's name is Martha. Their friends call them Charlie and Marti. I'm not quite sure how old they are, somewhere around 45, I guess. Pretty old. Dad's about my height, has a wide, barrel chest, and his hair's thinning. He's also getting some gray on his temples. Mom's shorter, thin, has dark brown hair and blue eyes.

I have a younger sister, Amy, 12. Five years younger. She's getting taller fast. She's blonde, skinny, awkward. She has brown eyes. She's starting seventh grade, but you know that. You have her in class, too.

I remember seventh grade. I was really scared of the seniors. In the halls they would knock the books out of our hands. We all held our books in front of us, like shields. I was excited about school then. We were sick of the grade school building and the teachers yelling at us all the time. Teachers here don't yell as much. That's nice.

I've been bored in school since then. You made English pretty interesting—as much as possible. That's why, when I needed an English course, I took one of yours. I don't like to read or write. All I can say is, I'm glad I have last hour study hall where I can write this garbage so I don't have to take it home.

There. I reached the end of my page. Good enough.

Tuesday: You were right. You didn't read our journals. You just glanced at them. It's really stupid, but it's an easy grade.

Today I'm sitting here not knowing what to write about.

My favorite class is building trades. We get to work on several projects for the whole semester. This year we're building a garage and then going to renovate a room in a nearby home.

I don't care for English or math. I'd rather be doing something with my hands. Because I took an extra Ag class last year I'm a half credit short of English. And because of that shortage, not only do I have to take journalism for the whole year but I also have to take a second English class next semester.

I used to like Ag classes. Those were my favorite classes, but this past summer changed that for me and my family. I remember hearing how 1984 was going to be such a weird year. People were expecting the world to end and stuff like that. It didn't end, except for us.

Since we sold the farm, it's too hard to take Ag. Sometimes I'm angry. Other times I'm sad.

I'd always planned to farm. Ever since I was little, my dad talked about us working together and how I would take over the farm someday. As far back as I can remember, I've known how to drive a tractor.

I miss the farm.

Now it's gone. The government took it.

It's been hard on us. My dad especially. We moved in August, when the corn was tall and full. Someone else will harvest it.

It's hard to live in town with all the noisy neighbors. The yards are so small. But it's good that we live close to school so I can walk. I had to sell my car to help with expenses. If we lived farther out, I'd have to ride the bus. Only little kids do that.

When I talked to Mr. Olson right before school started, he switched this year's Ag class to a math class. I guess that's good. I'm really rotten on my math.

My writing's not too hot either. What does this journal have to do with newspaper writing? It's stupid.

End of page. Good enough.

Wednesday: Plays? What can I write about plays? I've never even been to one. I could've written an article about football. Though my farm chores never let me be on the team, I've always been interested in it.

I understand that we have to write an article for the school newspaper, the *Hillcrest Gazette*, but you didn't have to give me this assignment.

I don't even know Miss Gunderson. What do I ask her? "What plays are you putting on this year?" Big deal. No one cares. That's not enough for a 200 word article.

So, Mrs. Webster, even though you don't read this, I'm getting my journal points by writing about how mad I am at you.

I suppose I'll talk to Miss Gunderson after school, see what she'd like to say.

It would've been easier with a different assignment. It'll be hard enough to put my writing in a good enough shape so I won't be embarrassed when people read it.

I'm close to the end of this page and still mad. Good enough. It'll have to do. If you want to dock me points, that's okay. I'm still mad at you, Mrs. Webster!

Thursday: I guess I owe you an apology, Mrs. W. The interview wasn't too bad. In fact, Miss Gunderson was very friendly and thanked me for the interview. Actually, she isn't too bad looking either. Her long dark brown hair curls nicely. She's kind of short, shorter than me anyway, and smiles pretty. I can see why a lot of the guys go out for the plays.

She even asked me if I would audition. Of course I said no. I've never done anything like that and don't want to.

They're doing *Arsenic and Old Lace* this fall. She said it's a really funny play and everyone would like it. But that stuff's all in the article.

I was surprised how much information she gave me, not only about the play but also about all the backstage workers she needs. The article wasn't hard to write. In fact, it was easy. You knew what you were doing after all, Mrs. W. I guess you usually do.

Though I'd never admit it to anyone, I was proud to see that article done. I'm glad I took typing class a few years ago so the article looked nice. I'm ashamed of my handwriting. I wish I could write neatly. I do wish I could write better. Maybe this class will help me.

I don't know what I'll do after graduation. Class of 1985. It used to seem so long ago. If I go on to any school, writing better will probably help. I wish I had planned ahead so I could go to college.

Looks like I went over my page a little.

Friday: Mrs. Webster, thanks for the list of ideas to write about in our journals. I hate to admit it, but I'm finding that the more I write, the easier it is to write. I also find that I'm not rushing through these journal entries, but I'm actually thinking a little as I write. topic: "Myself"

Chad Wilson. Age 17. I'm six feet, one inch. I don't think of myself as that tall, but that's what the tape measure says. Everyone I talk to, especially adults, seems bigger, even though I know I'm sometimes taller. (I wonder what the really tall guys like Steve Mifflin and Cliff Jorgenson think.)

I have medium brown hair. Mouse brown, my mother says. My eyes are blue. I have a little problem with zits, which I wish would clear up. Just when I think all is clear—BAM—a new zit.

My eyebrows are thick, too thick in the middle. My nose is

too big, so are my feet. I started to shave last year, every other day. I wish I had to shave every day. I guess I'm generally not happy with the way I'm made.

I wish I were more popular. I get along with the guys, but I get nervous and flustered when I talk to the girls. The pretty ones, that is. I don't date much. To be honest, not at all.

One good thing about me—The farm work has made me pretty strong. I know how to build things and I'm good with tools. One other thing—I'm honest. That's how I always got into trouble when I was a kid. I never could tell a believable lie. But I can't take credit for my honesty. My dad drove honesty into us with the same persistence he once drove in fence posts.

That's all there is to me, I guess. I'm not very important. I'm glad it's Friday.

Saturday: You said, Mrs. Webster, that we could write an extra credit journal entry over the weekend if we wanted to. So, here it is.

I'll write about one of those topics that you gave us: "My hometown":

Hillcrest. Second largest town in Ironwood County.

It's one of the highest points in southeastern Minnesota. To the east of town, large hills begin rolling all the way to the sheer bluffs along the Mississippi, some seventy miles away. To the west, flat fields of corn and soybeans stretch and stretch and stretch until they reach the Dakota plains.

Hillcrest's population is 1503. Most people have Scandinavian or German ancestors. We also have a small Hispanic migrant group that comes in the spring and leaves in the fall. They don't bother anyone else and no one bothers them.

Hillcrest High School draws the students from the town itself as well as those from nearby Oak Center, which isn't much more than a cluster of homes and a gas station. There's talk of a future consolidation with Cherry Grove as well as Paradise, a really small town to the northwest.

My graduating class numbers 106. I suppose we're a typical class. Not too much out of the ordinary happens in Hillcrest.

There. Extra credit. And, looking back, not too shabby writing either. I even threw in some extra descriptive words that you like, those adjectives.

Monday: For once I'm glad to be back in school. Dad wasn't his usual self this weekend. I guess he hasn't been for some time. Maybe his job at Johnson Brothers isn't going so well.

Anyway, he started yelling at Mom and then they got into a terrible fight. I'm not really sure what started it. I don't think Mom was sure either.

Amy and I escaped to our rooms, but I could still hear them. Dad's deep voice reverberated through the walls. It was silent for a moment, then Mom started shouting. I was shocked that Mom would argue back to Dad. She usually lets him walk all over her. Maybe she finally had enough. He yelled at her about cooking and then about how she never kept the place clean enough. She shouted back that he should get out of his chair and help her around the house.

"This house is your job," he bellowed. From my room, I pictured him towering over her.

I hate to hear them fight. Ever since our move, they fight more and more. I cried. I know guys aren't supposed to, but I did.

I know Amy did too. A lot. All weekend her eyes were red-rimmed and her lower lip quivered at times.

Later I mowed the lawn. I didn't need to, but I did anyway. It's the closest I can get to driving a tractor. Pathetic, ain't it?

Sunday we went to church. Dad didn't. He rarely does. Mom wore a smiling mask. She fooled most people, but Amy and I knew better. You can't fool family.

End of page. I'm glad you don't read these.

Tuesday: Things went better at home last night. Mom and Dad talked nicely to each other, trying to be polite. Too polite. It was obviously an effort.

Change subjects . . .

I think of tomorrow and I'm actually excited about my article coming out. I was proud of how it looked in the layout with my name under the headline. My first byline. What will people think about it when tomorrow's paper comes out? Who would've thought that a story by Chad Wilson would be printed?

(It's funny how this journal works. I usually don't know what to write, but once I start, it flows. I used to hate to write. Maybe that's because I didn't write and was afraid to try. Mrs. Webster says that writing is often like raising an iceberg: most of our ideas, like an iceberg, are under the surface of the water, but the act of writing brings the ideas to the surface where we can see them.)

My next news assignment is okay, a follow-up on the plays. Mrs. W. suggested that I get a detailed description of the major parts Miss Gunderson will be looking to fill. I'll try to see Miss G. tonight after school. I wouldn't mind a class from her sometime. Looking at her is easy on the eyes.

She doesn't look old enough to be a teacher. Mrs. Webster looks like a typical teacher with her primly cut, slightly gray hair and glasses. The sides of her blue eyes are a little wrinkled and she wears only a little make-up and she's a pinch fat. Is "plump" a better word?

But Miss Gunderson is another story. I've been noticing her in the hall. She walks nicely, with a little sway. Nice legs. Her make-up isn't too heavy, just right. I wonder if there's some guy in her life?

Just realized—what if I lost this journal? I better be careful what I write. After Mrs. W. glances at this entry, I better rip it out and throw it away at home.

Wednesday: Funny. I was going to destroy yesterday's page, but I didn't. I ripped it out and put it in my room. Even though I didn't want anyone to read the entry, I didn't want to throw it away. I've gone this far, I might as well keep recording what happens.

My article came out today. Bob Swanson said it was pretty good. It's exciting when other kids notice me.

I'm glad I took journalism instead of developmental reading.

I also talked—interviewed—Miss G. yesterday. She only had a few seconds before she had to dash off to some meeting. She gave me a list of characters. Today I need to ask her what she looks for in auditions.

She asked me again if I'd try-out. I said no. I think I blushed. I sure wouldn't mind working with her, but I couldn't get up in front of people.

Once in church I had to read some announcements as part of a "youth service." I was really nervous. When I think back on it, I feel that way again. At the time I sweat all over and my hands shook uncontrollably and my knees trembled the whole time. I lost my place half way through. I swore to myself—never again!

I did tell Miss G. that maybe I could help backstage with something. If she needed help, that is.

She smiled, said great. I know I glanced down.

Then again, maybe I better not help her. In the middle of some hammering I'd probably stare at her and smash my thumb.

Well, I'll get that information on auditions after school. You know, she must think I'm someone special to ask me to be in the plays.

I could write more, but I've math to do. End of page.

Thursday: Miss G. was still really nice but hurried through the information. Teachers must be busier than I thought. She had written down most of the audition information—I can stick the information right into my article. Talk about an easy piece of writing—all I had to do was type.

Miss G. has that nice flowery-looking handwriting that a lot of girls have. Why is my handwriting so lousy?

I told her again that I could maybe help her with the set. She asked me to consider being a stage manager.

"I'm not sure what they do," I said.

"They're in charge of everything during a production."

I didn't think I was up for that kind of responsibility and told her so. She just smiled and said auditions would be next week and she'd pick her cast and crew after that. I just had to let her know when I decided what I wanted to do.

Before this year I could never have been a stage manager or been involved in any extra-curricular activities because of my farm chores. I wonder—could I now? Would I? It scares me. I should talk to someone about it—maybe Mom.

But Mom has been weird lately. Even though she and Dad act better, some problem is still there, smoldering like a fire not quite out. What do parents do with a problem? Who do they talk to if not to each other?

Lately, things seem so disturbing, confusing.

I wish I could go back to our farm, sit on our high pasture hill and watch the cattle grazing below. It was always peaceful there. Quiet. The only sound was the wind blowing or a cow bellowing. I could see so far from that hill. In town I can't ever see the sun set.

Well, gotta work on my science lab report.

Not quite a page, but I've noticed Mrs. W. isn't too picky.

Friday: Seems like class work is worse then ever. I thought a person's senior year was supposed to be fun—not all these assignments.

It really makes me mad when teachers pile on the work, not realizing that other teachers are doing the same. They should make teachers coordinate plans and projects and tests so that assignments are staggered. Adults only have one employer—how come we have six?

I was called to the counselor's office today. He wanted me to transfer to a harder math class, said today was the last day to transfer, that he'd been looking over my aptitude tests and I could handle a greater challenge.

Sorry, I told him. I have enough challenge.

"What are your plans for next year?" he asked.

Seems like everyone is asking me that these days. Our youth pastor asked me the same thing last Sunday.

Are people required to ask seniors this question?

"I don't know," I told him.

I wish I did know.

Aaron Jones is going to the University, majoring in business. Decisions are easy for him. They always have been, even when we were little.

I remember playing with him in kindergarten. Even then he knew what he was going to do. I just tagged along.

Ever since he started dating Jennifer Grigson, I don't see much of him anymore. Is he getting serious about her?

Seems, though, like most of the heavy dating couples (those who are always together and you're sure are going to get married the day after graduation) break up before college. That's what happened to Betty Kohl. She hung onto Wayne Anderson, assuming he'd give her a ring at graduation. Instead, he went off to college and met new people.

What's it like to date that much? I've always been awkward around girls. In the past I was also so busy with the farm that I never seemed to have time for anything else. At least, it was a convenient excuse.

Funny, I actually enjoy writing in this journal. I discover all sorts of things about myself.

An iceberg rising to the surface.

Monday: Study hall's empty today. Some kids are absent and some signed out for the library.

I like the quiet.

When I think of quiet, I think of our hill west of our old farmhouse where I used to sit after a hard, hot day of working on the farm. There always seemed to be a cool evening breeze on that hill, and it always felt good. I often watched the cattle grazing in the pasture below. The land beyond our fence stretched west all the way to the horizon. The fall was a great time to see brilliant sunsets.

But no use dwelling on the past. The farm is gone. The hill is gone. The violet sunsets are gone.

Tension at home. Lots of it.

Dad quit his job at Johnson Brothers, saying he had enough of mindless assembly work.

"Why didn't you wait until you had a new job lined up?" Mom asked him. I noticed Mom's hands trembling as she ran a hand over her dark hair.

"The foreman—the little mustached squirt—was pushing his weight around and I had it. I told him what I thought of his stupid job and walked out."

Mother cried a lot this weekend.

I tried to talk to her on Sunday. Though I've always had my doubts, she has a lot of faith in prayer and God. I told her to really pray about it, that we could all pray about it. She cried a little harder and then hugged me. After she dried her eyes, she cheered up a bit. She quoted the Bible, about how all things work together for good and all that.

She's always had a strong faith, taking us to Sunday school and vacation Bible school and youth activities. I've always listened, but it has never quite made sense to me. Maybe I'll have to figure it out for myself someday.

Amy goes to all the church activities, but I think she likes the social part of it more than the religious. Dad sure doesn't put much stock in God, even less when the farm went under.

I know Aaron Jones doesn't attend church. His goal in life is to make money. Lots of it.

I hope Dad has spent the day looking for a job and not sitting around watching TV.

Tuesday: I'm writing this during the last few minutes of journalism class.

New assignment—work with another student on an editorial. I couldn't believe the partner that Mrs. W. assigned me—Melanie Johnson! I'm really nervous. I've had a crush on her since second grade. After school we're supposed to meet to brainstorm in the journalism room.

More on that tomorrow. Right now, I better get my mind off her. Idea from list: "Description"

The grassy field out the window is green.

Dumb. Try again.

Looking out the window, the trees—how can trees look? Dumb.

The mid-morning sun casts the slim tree shadows across the field of grass. Better.

Sitting in the pale green journalism room, I look out the large window. The mid-morning sun, already bringing warm hints of the heat to come, casts slender tree shadows across the field of grass. Beyond is a metal wire fence. Beyond that runs a row of small homes. A slight breeze, a dry autumn breeze, slips into the open window and ruffles papers along the table.

A few students mill around the room, conversing in low murmurs about the weekend, about articles, about classes and teachers. Most are busy writing, if not future articles, then in their journals. A few who have worked ahead in journalism hastily finish a different class's assignment before the bell.

How's that, Mrs. W.? Maybe I'll show that part to you to get your opinion.

Looking back, I don't know if I like it. It doesn't sound like me: "hints of the heat to come" sounds phony. Artificial. I don't think I'd even like it in a book.

Well, I better jot down some ideas before my afternoon meeting with Melanie. My hands feel sweaty already.

Wednesday: Was I nervous yesterday after school! She wore her long light brown hair pulled back, accentuating her high cheekbones and large blue eyes. She's a little shorter than I—and what a body!

(I don't know if that's good descriptive writing or not—with her I lose my concentration!)

We talked about possible editorials. She sat kind of close. I could almost feel the heat from her (from my?) body.

She's really bright and outgoing, and she smiles a lot with perfect, white teeth. One can't help but be happier around her.

We finally settled on the consolidation issue. Actually, Cherry Grove would be joining our school district. We'll examine the pro's and con's—I'll take the con's. She'll take the positive things. We'll both interview people separately and write the rough draft on Monday. We have plenty of time—two weeks. Shouldn't be too bad—not with Melanie as a partner.

It's funny how things work out. We've known each other since kindergarten but never talked, nothing beyond pleasantries. Yesterday, though, we talked easily, like old friends. I think she dates quite a bit. Too bad. It'd be hard to get her to go out with me. Besides, she's part of the higher class—football cheerleader and volleyball player, now up for homecoming queen.

Of the three social classes at Hillcrest, I'm definitely not in the upper one.

Almost forgot! The school paper came out today. I received several good comments about my article. Miss G. saw me in the hall and thanked me. Get that! I was thanked for doing an assignment. She sure is nice. I think I will sign up for stage crew.

Thursday: Chemistry is getting harder. Trig is too. Glad I didn't transfer into a harder math class. Maybe I should've taken a foreign language instead. Well, I'll never go to a different country. But then, I'll never use this math either. Government class is really boring. I better decide on my term paper topic. I still enjoy building trades—it's practical and useful.

Mom asked me this morning about my plans for next year. I think she's worried about me. That makes two.

Living in town has been difficult—trying to ignore the noisy neighbors, learning to pull shades, remembering to lock doors. I have no chance to go outside and be alone, really alone.

I miss the pasture and the hill and the sunsets. I could think clearly there. Everything was certain and reliable and sure.

I know Mom misses the farm too.

She used to walk evenings along the grove. She can still walk, of course, but she has to talk to all the neighbors along the way.

I wonder if it's worse in the Twin Cities? Or are there so many people that you can't really be friendly, so why bother? Maybe that's solitude in the crowd instead of in the country.

Anyway, I'm worried about her. She doesn't have her same drive or happiness. I know Dad's dragging her down.

Occasionally Amy tries to help, but she's so flighty. I guess most seventh graders are. I'm glad Amy's gone out for volleyball. Her height will help her. It also keeps her busy and out of my hair.

I'm glad Dad keeps looking for a job. The last thing Mom needs is Dad hanging around the house all day. If that happened, she'd go out and find a job. That'd be hard on him too, almost as hard as losing the farm. The last remnant of the old farm life would be gone.

I remember how Dad worked me hard, worked himself hard too, but it was good work. Even though sweat would be running down our heads and necks and chests like rivers, we knew that what we were doing was important.

We've sure changed since we moved from the farm. It's already hard to remember our old white farmhouse or the grove I played in as a kid or even the dusty haymow. It's like a dream mostly forgotten.

Sometimes I hurt inside.

Friday: I called several people in Cherry Grove. Residents there have mixed feelings about consolidating with us. The mayor is against it. Strongly. Bad for business, he thought. On the other hand, the city clerk thought consolidation would help because people from Hillcrest might shop more in Cherry Grove. Cherry Grove, as a tourist town, draws a lot of summer travelers but not many county visitors. The president of the student council was for it. (I didn't like him. Of course I only talked to him on the phone, but he came across as arrogant.) Their senior class president was friendly. She didn't know if a bigger school necessarily meant better.

It was a good question. Right now, Hillcrest High School is still "B" size. Bringing in Cherry Grove would make us a size larger. In athletics we would play larger schools. Before Hillcrest and Cherry Grove would actually consolidate, we'd pair for a few years. Can a paired school compete effectively with a larger town school—a school all under one roof?

I have lots of notes for Monday's meeting with Melanie. I also signed up with Miss G. this morning. Funny how last year, girls didn't exist, and this year I've encountered two beauties— Melanie and Miss G—and I'm on speaking terms with both.

I'm going to the football game tonight with Aaron and Jennifer. I don't like to be a tag-along but without a car I have no choice. I'm sure Jennifer will hate to have me with, and, as usual, she'll be rude and crabby. I wonder what he sees in her?

Monday: topic: "recreated dialogue"

Melanie and I sat next to each other at the long table. A typewriter sat near each end. She was excited. Her high cheeks were flushed and her blue eyes nearly sparkled.

"So many positive things," she bubbled. "More kids, more class choices, greater selection of teachers, more extra-curricular activities. Even hockey would be possible."

"Is what we have now bad?" I asked. Her enthusiasm dwindled and she appeared offended. "A larger school is not necessarily better," I stated, "just larger. We need to consider what we would gain compared to what we would lose."

"Such as?" Her initial bewilderment turned into hostility. Her smile had vanished and she folded her arms and crossed her legs. But I couldn't, or wouldn't, back down.

"In a few years, we could become double-A size, competing against schools far larger. Can we compete against Edina in hockey?"

"Northern schools do."

"So does Rochester. They have year-round arenas. We don't." I paused and restated my opinion. "My point is that we must consider what we'd lose." I took a deep breath and continued. "Secondly, do we need more class choices? All the basics and almost all of the options are available. Some extra languages might be added, but we do have Spanish."

An almost tangible anger smoldered in her large blue eyes.

"So you're set against it?"

"Not necessarily. Let's consider both sides in our editorial, without prejudice, and try to reach a conclusion."

She sighed and unfolded her arms and leaned back. "So, you think I'm prejudiced?"

I hedged. "No. You've reached your conclusion based on what you considered. I have other points to consider too."

"I'll write the beginning," she said stiffly, formally, and flipped her hair back. "You find a typewriter and write the middle. Start with something like 'But the other side must be considered as well.' Or along those lines."

"Fine," I said, and tried to smile . . . .

I tried to write that dialogue just as it happened this morning. She was cold towards me the rest of the period: as my grandfather often says, as cold as a Minnesota outhouse in January. We did finish the two parts and merge them adequately, but we didn't reach any satisfying conclusion.

Tomorrow we'll show the editorial to Mrs. W. for her advice. It's too bad.

I guess we didn't make such good partners.

Tuesday: After school, at home:

Two important things to write about today. First, Dad got a job. I'm not sure I'll like it, but he's looking forward to starting it Monday. He'll be a custodian at school.

What will I do if I see him in the halls? Do I smile, "Hi, Dad," or do I act nonchalantly, or do I look away? How will he act?

Come to think of it—he could check up on my classes pretty easily. What'll the teachers say about me? I guess I shouldn't be too worried—I'm pretty inconspicuous.

I'll find out next week if his job will be good or bad for me.

Second news. Mrs. W. thought Melanie and I covered the topic thoroughly in our editorial. She said it was good that we came to an end, not a definitive conclusion, and Mrs. Webster added that the issue was indeed not clear-cut. We did the right thing by avoiding a hasty, easy resolution. She said we were very wise to recommended further study and "careful consideration before deciding."

She felt Melanie and I worked together perfectly. She's assigning us another joint editorial for the next issue.

Melanie wasn't too happy about working with me again. When Mrs. W. was talking to us, Melanie just stared out the window, almost pouting. Was Melanie expecting Mrs. W. to cut me down?

If so, I should be really disgusted at Melanie's childish attitude. So what if she didn't get her way? We did get a better editorial. It seems to me that doing the job right is important, not how we get there or who is right or wrong along the way.

I'm sure not mad at her. I want to work with her again. Ever since grade school, I've thought she was so pretty that I was afraid to talk to her. I'm not afraid anymore. And I still think that Melanie's long hair and blue eyes and high cheekbones and shapely figure make her the most beautiful girl in school.

Wednesday: Dad had a meeting with the head custodian today. When Dad got home, he told us how impressed he was with the building and said that the school district would send him to school to get his boiler operator's license. From then on, things deteriorated. topic: "recreated dialogue"

"We can be so thankful for the job," Mom said as she brought the roast to the table.

The rest of us had already sat down. Dad's voice suddenly became edged with sarcasm.

"Thankful?"

Mom immediately knew something was wrong when he hit his argumentative "I dare you" voice, but she wouldn't back down.

"Thankful to the Lord for this job," she stated.

"What's God got to do with this?" he snapped. "I had to find it."

"Yes, dear." She smiled, but her hands trembled as she adjusted the plate with the roast in the center of the table. She pulled her hands back into her lap as she sat down. "Amy, why don't you scoop up some mashed potatoes for Chad?"

Amy threw her head back. "He doesn't need any help."

I know Amy is dense, but I didn't fully realize how thick until that moment. Mom was just trying to divert attention from her hands.

I jumped in: "Of course I don't need any help." My voice was too nervous and too boisterous as I reached for the potatoes.

Puzzled, Amy glanced at me, frowning, really shocked that I wouldn't insist on being waited on as Dad often does. I refused to give her the satisfaction of an argument on male-female roles. Looking directly at her, I grinned across the table.

Dad, however, wasn't diverted by our exchange.

"God this and God that," he mimicked cruelly. "Did God save our farm?"

"Not in front of the children," Mom said meekly, adding, as an afterthought, "dear." She hastily put some meat on Dad's plate.

"You talk about God in front of them and cart them off to church. Why not let them hear some other side?"

Amy, pale, stared at her plate. She also had lost her appetite. Both of us wanted to crawl away from the table.

"Well, let's eat, and at least try to be pleasant," Mom said. Flushed, she slipped her trembling hands back under the table.

Dad glanced at us and finally realized how we were feeling. He paused and looked down for a minute thoughtfully. He rubbed his chin. He was as guilty as a wolf with a sheep in his belly, and he knew it.

My whole life I don't think I've ever heard him say he was sorry and I don't think I ever will.

He leaned back from the table, and, like some medieval king, announced his decree: "Yes, we can be pleasant, even if we disagree." Then he reached forward and scooped up a big wad of mashed potatoes. He continued to sermonize. "I've always appreciated honesty in a person. Forthrightness. I was just expressing my opinion. We need to express our thoughts more. That's what's wrong with this country."

He leaned toward me a bit, looking for support. "Right, Chad?"

"Right," I said, rather softly, then took a mouthful of potatoes.

The problems—whatever they are—existing between Mom and Dad stretch longer than the Mississippi. They must be rooted in more than just the job or the farm. It must be hard for two people to always live together and to be happy, but if they love each other, they can work it out. And they must love each other. They did get married after all.

Thursday: It helps to write. I don't know why, but I feel better by writing about my family's problems.

Maybe it's like talking to a friend. I've never had many really close friends. Aaron was, but since last year he sees Jennifer all the time. Yet when I think back, we never did that many things outside of school. I've always been a loner. topic: "description of friend"

Aaron Jones. Just turned 18. A little shorter than I am—a little under six feet tall. He is skinny with a very triangular face and pointy chin. His brown curly hair gives him a carefree, innocent look. I remember many times he misbehaved in school and the teachers never suspected him. Somehow he always gets away with everything.

Aaron has a good sense of humor and an easy disposition— like me in that way. We'll take what life dishes out to us without complaining.

I have never seen him depressed.

His biggest fault is that he lets Jennifer run his life. She makes many of his decisions, where to go and what to see, even whom (did you catch that good grammar?) to talk to. She's about 5'6" with brown wavy hair. She's not a real beauty, for her face is too thin, but she does have nice bright green eyes and an attractive figure.

If she had a better personality, I'd be jealous.

Aaron and Jennifer will get married after graduation if she has her way, after college if he has his. He knows how hard college can be if a person's married—his older brother tried it and got divorced after two years.

Will they be happily married? How long can he tolerate her decision-making? Her tyranny? If he does finally take charge, can she tolerate it? Some girls like to control a guy, others like the guy to take the lead. Girls are as variable as guys, I guess. It seems to me that it would be best to have a balance of some sort . . . but what do I know?

I know Mom likes Dad to be in charge as long as he is civil and respects her opinion. Lately, though, he's gone too far and she's chafing a bit . . . no, a lot.

Seems to me that getting married must be a pretty tough decision, one of the most important decisions a person ever makes. It's frightening.

Friday: Mom and Dad were much better last night and they talked civilly to each other at breakfast. On Monday Dad will start work at school. I decided that I won't walk to school anymore but will ride with him at 7 a.m. If I get to school that early, it'll force me to get all my studying done.

Miss Gunderson caught me in the hall this morning and asked if I would be stage manager. I said I really didn't know if I could, that I didn't know anything about plays.

"This'll be a great way to learn."

What could I say? She smiled that big, optimistic, happy smile of hers. I shrugged and said okay.

Mrs. W. announced in class that today's journal entry is the last one required. I have mixed feelings about it. I remember how I thought it was so stupid. Now, after four weeks, writing's become a sort of habit . . . or maybe more, like scratching an itch. Not that I have an itch to write, but it helps me to think through things, to sort things out. Maybe writing, as Mrs. W says, is a kind of thinking. I still picture that iceberg coming to surface. I see more of it all the time. I understand my thoughts and feelings better if I see them.

Anyway, because she's assigned us to yearbook duties, she won't require the journal entries. We can write them, though, for a little extra credit. Maybe I'll keep the journal going and show it to her at the end of the quarter. With an eighth of my senior year done, it'd be a shame to end this record here. Besides, I could use the extra credit.

End of page. That's enough.

* * * Extra credit entries * * *

Monday: topic: "senior reflections"

Hillcrest is a nice school to attend. It's small when compared to a city school, but large when compared to closer small town schools—like Paradise—which have hung onto their separate identities past their time.

I'm glad I've attended Hillcrest, for it's given me a well-rounded education. I've learned a little of everything and more about some things than I care to know. Though I've often complained, I can look back as a senior and see it's been good.

Reading my past journal entries, I can see how much I've changed in such a short time. In the beginning, I hated to write. Now I choose to write. Attitudes can really make a difference. Maybe attitudes are the key ingredient to success.

Something else is weird. Thinking back to those first four weeks of school, I don't recall most of the things I wrote about. I remember some of the big things—my first article getting printed in the paper, thinking Miss G. has great legs (she still does), working with Melanie, and tense times at home. But that's about all. Everything blurs together. I'm glad I have these things recorded so that I know that they happened. They're like snapshots of each day.

So much of life speeds by and escapes my notice or is lost from my memory. I don't have the time to really see events before they're gone.

(Could I do an editorial on that?)

Maybe I have to seize more initiative. I only have one senior year. Next year who knows where I'll be.

Tuesday: Melanie is still unfriendly. We've begun work on a new editorial about how well schools prepare (or don't prepare) students for the job market.

I hope we'll agree on this editorial. I like talking to her, like working with her, and, to be honest, like looking at her.

The cast of *Arsenic and Old Lace* started play practice tonight. I sat in on the read-through. It's a very funny play, but I didn't have much to do. Miss G. said that after tonight I could skip several weeks until they get through all the blocking and the interruptions of homecoming week.

After homecoming I'll need to regularly attend rehearsals. I wish Melanie was in the play, but she's already too busy with cheerleading and volleyball.

Dad and Mom are still acting cordially to each other. Almost too congenial. As if both are trying too hard. Dad likes his job and I really don't see him very often at school. We talk a little on the way to school, as much as he ever talks to me.

I'm really tired. I wonder if all play rehearsals last this long. I ache all over.

Friday: Sick two days with the flu. I had really strange dreams, all about eating and drinking. Must've been really hungry.

I wish I could've kept my journal going when I was sick.

Already I've forgotten how lousy I felt, the awful sensations, the aching head.

On second thought, maybe it's good I've forgotten.

I wonder how different this journal would be if I wrote one week at a time? Though I'm sure it would be more coherent, I would really lose a lot of the individual moments.

The class work is piled high tonight with make-up assignments. Got to cut short the journal.

Monday: Homecoming week. Everyone's excited about the big volleyball game and bonfire on Tuesday, the coronation Thursday, the game Friday. For our class's skit we're doing a take-off on *The Twilight Zone.* Rod Serling (Bob Swanson) is the narrator of a "twilight zone" encounter between the Hillcrest Rangers and the Cherry Grove Wildcats. Bob came up with the idea. He should know what he's doing—he's been in all the plays since ninth grade.

The candidate choices were all pretty predictable. I knew Bob S. would be nominated for king. (But I'm hoping Steve Mifflin will get it. Though we haven't ever been close friends, we've always attended the same church and he's always been friendly to me, friendly to everyone. He's the nicest person I know.) After the first popularity contest in seventh grade, the celebrities of the class became pretty much set, if not in concrete, then at least in everyone's minds—which may be even harder than a concrete slab. You're either one of the elite or you're not. I suppose that's true of all classes. Maybe true of all schools. (If true, that's very sad, not because I'm not one of the elite, but because it says something about our inability to change. Or an unwillingness. Either way, it doesn't reflect well on human nature.)

Melanie, of course, is one of the queen candidates. She'll look stunning on Thursday. Miss G. asked if I'd help backstage Thursday night.

"Glad to," I said. It'll be the best place to be—that way I'll have an excuse not to be in the senior skit (if they even ask me).

Aaron and I plan to go to the volleyball game tomorrow. He strongly hinted that I was on my own after the game. He and Jennifer are staying for the bonfire, then driving out to Swanson's. Must be a party there. He didn't offer to give me a ride there, not that I was invited.

I suppose I'll go to the bonfire and then walk home. I miss having a car of my own. It was hard when I had to sell it. I hate to ask Dad all the time to borrow his. When we lived on the farm, I'd earn enough money during the summer to afford a car, insurance, and gas for the rest of the year.

Even if I do borrow Dad's car, it's not the same as driving my own.

Tuesday: An unusual evening.

First, we lost the game. The volleyball team played poorly and some of the girls were mad at the others. Melanie and several others—including Jennifer—glared furiously at Janet Nelson and Lisa Overlund whenever they missed a spike or set (which happened quite often). The other girls' timing was off too.

The coach was steaming on the sidelines. She was constantly pacing along the bench and twice threw her clipboard down. Two starters played terribly and the rest of the team, rather than working together, was pulling apart.

Afterwards, everyone went outside to the empty lot next to the school where the student council had piled dry brush and old lumber for the bonfire.

The fire was already blazing.

Someone had set it on fire during the last period of the game. The crowd was disappointed and angry. From now on they'll have to put a guard near the pile. Knowing administrators' thinking, though, they'll just abolish the bonfire completely.

Aaron and I were watching the fire die into embers when Jennifer, Melanie, and Sarah Webster walked up. I could see their anger from a distance.

"Too bad about the game," Aaron sympathized.

Light from the embers lit Melanie's face with a beautiful, flickering red glow.

"And too bad about the fire," I added awkwardly. The three girls turned to me. "Someone lit it early," I explained. They were so furious about something that they hadn't seemed to notice. Nor, I realized, did they care.

"Oh," said Melanie.

"How are you guys?" asked Sarah, trying to cheer up and change the subject. Sarah's really a nice girl, (Don't you think so, Mrs. W.?) a junior, dark hair, dark eyes, tall and graceful.

"Okay," we muttered.

Jennifer shifted next to Aaron, clutching his arm.

"Well," Aaron finally asked, "what happened to the team?"

Melanie crossed her arms. "It didn't help that two of our starters and a sub were half-drunk." She glared at the fading red glow of the fire.

"Really?" I blurted. I knew lots of guys drank but I always assumed the girls were pretty clean. All eyes turned toward me and I blushed. I had just revealed to the three girls my general ignorance. I guess I am pretty sheltered—my parents never drink (well, my dad has a beer or two on the Fourth of July) and I've never had any alcohol (except for some sips he used to give me.)

Sarah, perhaps sensing my embarrassment, stepped closer to me. "We never expected someone to drink before a game either. They were a little odd in school today, but no one put it together. They bragged in the locker room about how they partied last night and will all week."

Everybody complained about them for a few minutes.

"Well," I finally said, doing my best to sound positive, "maybe they learned a lesson and won't do it again."

"That's just it," said Melanie. "They didn't learn. It's a big joke to them."

I wondered if it truly was. Perhaps they had to make it a joke in order to hide their deep shame.

"Well," said Aaron, pulling Jennifer away with him, "we better be going."

Just then a car drove into the parking lot and honked. Melanie turned to the car, a white Pontiac. "There's Jay. Gotta go."

Suddenly I was deserted, except for Sarah. I didn't know what to say.

"Are you going to Swanson's too?" she asked.

"No." I glanced down, shoving my hands into my jacket pockets. "I walked tonight." I didn't add that I no longer had a car of my own. "I live in town now. It's so close."

"Oh," she said. "I usually walk too, only four blocks away." Long pause.

"Well, seeing how we're both walking," I finally said. "Mind if I walk with you?"

"Okay," she said and zipped up her coat. "It's getting chilly."

"Good dry night for the corn," I said as we began walking home.

We talked about a lot of things in those four blocks. We even talked a few minutes while standing on her sidewalk. Nothing important, but she's easy to talk to. She's a nice girl.

I guess I already said that.

Wednesday: Melanie, wearing a dress because of homecoming week, and I were standing outside the darkroom discussing our editorial. Suddenly she slipped her hand around my arm and glided us into the darkroom. She shut the door behind us and put her hands around my neck. I reached around her waist and pulled her close.

We kissed. A long time. She raised her leg, brought it around mine, and I ran my hand along her thigh, up her dress.

Suddenly (as things do in dreams) we were elsewhere, in a field somewhere near a burning bonfire and she had her clothes off though I couldn't really see her.

Then I woke, feeling both tired and excited. I got up and went to the bathroom.

I hate those dreams, yet find them exciting too.

Everyone says they're normal, but I don't know why I feel weird and sick afterwards. Way back in junior high our youth pastor had a special class for the boys. I remember him talking about it and yet he never said that they happen more often as you get older. Now that we're older, nobody talks about it at all.

Maybe that's why I feel weird. It's never talked about, so, we conclude, it must be bad. Sex education comes too early to really understand, and when you finally are old enough to understand, everyone figures you know it all already.

It seems that most of what kids know comes from the movies. I guess deep down, I'm glad I'm normal. It's confusing.

What's the difference between love and lust?

Thursday: Tonight's homecoming coronation went really well. Backstage was fun. I ran the lights as well as the curtain. Miss G. would come backstage every so often to see how things were going. She was operating the P.A. system out front.

Our skit was a riot. Bob Swanson was a real ham tonight. He can get away with things that others never could. The way he exaggerated his voice and face was amazing.

The seniors won second place in the skit contest, though. The juniors got first. They usually do. Since juniors sponsor homecoming, the judges pat them on the back with a little trophy. I remember winning last year, how proud I felt, even though I'd only had a small, non-speaking part standing in a group

During coronation, all the candidates filed by me—once when being introduced, a second time during the actual coronation. The girls looked fantastic—especially Melanie. She had on a blue shoulderless dress with white ruffles on the bottom. Her hair was flowing down the back of her long neck. She looked so— ("old" isn't the right word)—mature.

Sarah was there, too. I'd forgotten that she was a junior candidate. (Seems like teachers' kids often are in the running.)

The guys looked nice—actually sophisticated—in tuxedos. Back stage, before being introduced, several made crude jokes to each other in a nervous sort of way. So much for the mature, cultured look. Steve Mifflin, his usual self, just stood quietly off to the side.

Right before the actual crowning, Melanie sidled close to me. I don't think she knew I was there by the stage curtains, for when I said "Good Luck," I startled her.

She glanced at me. "Thanks, Chad," she said and stared out onto the stage again. Then, without warning, she grabbed my arm, squeezed it, and my pulse raced. Next she nervously fiddled with her gloves. Even over her perfume, I smelled her strong breath, which surprised me. Sort of acidic.

All the seniors were on stage when they announced the queen. Melanie, of course.

I was really happy for her and jealous that I couldn't stand beside her. Bob Swanson did.

Friday: Special issue of the paper came out today on all the extra-curricular activities with, of course, special emphasis on football. I had written two articles. One was a profile of Steve Mifflin, the quiet wide receiver, and one on *Arsenic and Old Lace* (am I type cast, or what? How's that for a double pun? Type? Cast?)

At supper Dad complained about coronation yesterday: What a mess it was to clean up. Kids had thrown crepe paper, programs, gum wrappers and assorted junk from the skits all over the gym and stage.

I hope Dad doesn't get to be like some of the other janitors. All they do is gripe. The teachers hate to hear griping. Kids hate to hear griping too, at least from adults. We expect it from ourselves.

Dad, Mom, and I had talked earlier about us going to the game as a family. After all, Dad was an alumni. After we ate, I reminded him.

"No," he said. "I've had enough of school things."

"But this is different," I persisted. "You don't have to go as part of your job. It's homecoming. Didn't you and Mom meet at a game?"

"That was basketball," Dad said.

Mom didn't sound like she wanted to go either. "It's going to be chilly tonight."

Oh well, that was that. I tried.

At least Dad gave me the car tonight. I didn't need it but it was nice to drive to the game, stand around the car, and shoot the breeze with the guys.

Amy tagged along but she quickly disappeared with her seventh grade friends. The night was, as Mom said, chilly—a nice fall evening for a football game. I sat by Aaron and Jennifer. She was hanging all over him. He sure didn't seem to mind.

Aaron and I used to do so many things together. I don't see us doing much in the future. I guess high school friends stay pretty much that—high school friends. Once you graduate, you leave those friends and find new ones.

Melanie sat with the cheerleaders up front, near some really tall, blond guy with a Cherry Grove letter jacket. It looked like Jay MacNeil, the guy who is supposedly so good in basketball that the basketball coach wouldn't let him go out for football.

Last night I was jealous of Bob Swanson. Now it was Jay MacNeil.

At half time the royalty rode around the infield and the band performed a half time routine.

I had a shock a little after half time. Mom and Dad came and brought a thermos of hot chocolate. As soon as I spotted them, I stood and waved them over. As they worked their way through the crowded bleachers, Aaron and Jennifer made room, quite a bit in fact, and she quit pawing him.

It was really great that Dad and Mom came.

"I used to bring you to these games when you were little, remember?" he said.

I did. Half the time I was freezing and he'd wrap me in one of those red-plaid, wool stadium blankets. I'd spend most of my time sipping hot chocolate instead of watching the game, not that I understood any of it then anyway.

Hillcrest won the game. Dad was going to drive, then remembered who brought the car. I drove us all home.

A good week.

Monday: Mrs. Webster says a good writer writes and keeps writing, but the teachers, after easing up on the assignments last week, are now making up for lost time. The workload is really piling up.

How does a writer write when there's no time to write? Right?

Tuesday: The play has some really funny spots. Bob Swanson (Mortimer) is great. Steve Mifflin was talked into the part of the killer, Jonathan. He looks good in the part but seems pretty stiff. I can't think of a nicer guy to play a killer. Did Miss G. know what she was doing? I've known Steve a long time through church and he's always been quiet and reserved, not one to throw himself into a part. I hope he can relax and play it up more.

It's funny how I'm learning by watching others act. Well, it's late—no more time.

Wednesday: In my bedroom:

Sore neck from sanding sheet rock on the ceiling in building trades class.

I wonder how long a person can last hanging sheet rock? I know they make great money, but do they have to take welfare at age 30 because their body is wrecked? I really like working on these projects but I can't see keeping it up 8-10 hours a day, year after year.

Mom gave me some aspirin. Going to bed early.

No school tomorrow or Friday because of teachers' meetings. I just have play practice Thursday morning and then I'll catch up on my sleep.

Thursday: In my bedroom:

Just got home from a special 3-hour play practice—Phew! A very busy week is over—and it was a short week too—only 3 days and one extra rehearsal. I think my head is still spinning from all the assignments. And just when I get everything done it's off to play practice. These plays take a lot of work . . . and it's still five weeks to go.

My job as stage manager is now to follow the book for Miss G. She said that she'll alternate me with the other tech people so that they're also familiar with the play. For the next few weeks I'll have a lighter schedule.

"Oh," she added, "be ready to step into a part too. We never know when someone gets sick."

Great. Just great. She never told me that before. Understudy, she called it.

Just what I need. Another thing to worry about.

Saturday: It's difficult living in town. Today Dad and I watched college football games on TV. Neither of us said it, but we both missed the farm. The area farmers all had bumper crops this year.

Sitting indoors is hard when you could be outside in the cool autumn air, smell the dry husks and the grain dust. Seeing hard work amount to something helps you to plant again. It teaches you the value of picking rock and pulling weeds. Walking beans wasn't so bad. In fact, when Dad got the rider a few years ago, that job lost something.

He had bought quite a bit of new farm equipment in the years just before we lost the farm. That was part of the problem.

Money out. Not enough money in. And the bank holding all the strings.

I used to be puzzled when other kids who didn't live on a farm would talk about this or that television show. I rarely watched TV. We rarely had time. I've seen more TV since living in town than I watched in my all my previous years combined.

So Dad sat on the sofa, I lay on the floor. We had root beer and popcorn. At half time we went outside and cut back the shrubs.

In town, I can't see the sun rise or set. People are all around.

I remembered again how, after checking cattle, I would sit on the hillside and look west across the fields to the distant farms and the endless horizon.

I can see why so many town people, as soon as summer comes, pack up and drive to a cabin on a lake. They need to get away from other people and to be outside. In town, they don't get to be outside, not really outside. A fenced in backyard doesn't count for much.

Sunday: Our church, steeple-topped, white, and a century-old, sits on the first hill north of Hillcrest. In the fall, the maple trees around it show off brilliant yellow and orange leaves. In winter the snow drifts down the steeple and onto the roof. White mounds of snow crown the surrounding trees. Our church in winter always reminds me of a Christmas card.

Behind the church, a low metal fence surrounds an old cemetery. Most of my ancestors on my father's side are buried there.

Today, as we walked through the main double oak doors and made our way to the steps leading to the balcony, our youth pastor caught up with me.

Pastor Jim was flushed. His red face almost matched his red hair. He must have run up from Sunday school.

"Chad," he blurted and then suddenly acted nonchalant. I could tell he had rushed to catch me. "We've missed you in Sunday school."

How could he have missed me? I haven't gone since seventh grade. Morning chores on the farm always lasted through Sunday school. I didn't know how to reply.

Ahead of me, going up the creaky oak stairs to the balcony, my mom paused.

I might as well be honest, I thought. "Amy's made it," I stammered. "But I've always been busy." Then I could have kicked myself—I buckled under pressure. I faltered. I hesitated. I glanced down. "It's hard to get in the habit. I'll see if I can make it next week."

I must've made his morning, for his face lit up. "That's great," he said. "But I also wanted to let you know that we're planning a fall retreat for our senior high. We'll be going up to camp the second weekend in November. If you're interested we must know next week and you need to turn in a $5 deposit."

Mom came down the steps. Over my shoulder she piped in. "Chad, if you want to go." She didn't say anything more but began digging in her purse.

Caught between, I thought.

"I'll think about it," I said quickly and touched Mom's hand.

"Great," Pastor Jim said and then he was gone, cheerfully greeting some other people coming in.

Yeah, I thought. Great.

Why me?

Monday: Today I felt tired all day. Classes dragged.

During lunch, Bob Swanson announced that he was planning a big Halloween party at his house. Looking around the table, he included everyone in his invitation. He glanced over at me.

"Chad, you didn't make it to the homecoming party." He grinned his politician's smile. "Can't miss this one."

"Oh," I said, surprised. I hadn't been asked to any homecoming party. It shows you where I rate on the social register.

I shouldn't wonder, though, at my lack of social status. Dad always kept us busy on the farm so I never had a chance to be involved. Even if I had been invited in earlier years, I probably couldn't have gone. I wouldn't have felt comfortable. At least I can tell myself that. It's a good excuse.

Tuesday: I worked on the set after school today alongside Miss G. and a handful of other stage workers. Even in a long shop coat and jeans, she looked great.

When I first arrived on stage, I stood around, not sure what to do. Her play production class had already erected the wall pieces—"flats" they're called.

"Chad," she said, walking over to me. "Could you make me a sturdy railing for these steps?"

"Sure," I said. I studied the situation—two flights of steps. The upper set rested on a 4-foot high wood platform and led off behind a flat. The upper flight ended backstage—8 feet off the stage floor.

"How do they get off?" I asked.

"I thought we'd make another platform or some steps leading down."

I had helped Dad move a few things around the school and knew what would work. "Why not use the old scaffolding down near the boiler room?"

Her eyes brightened. "I didn't know there was any. Do you think we could use it?"

"I'll ask Dad. I'm sure its okay."

If we hadn't been in school, I'm sure she would've hugged me.

In two hours, we had the scaffolding up (with Dad's help) and I had her railing made.

She stood on the top flight, the stage lights brightening her long dark hair, and admired my handiwork. "The best thing I ever did," she said when we were done, "was ask you to be stage manager."

I held back my smile, scrutinized the set, and nodded approvingly.

Wednesday: Things are so busy. Seems like I just run and do something quickly and then run to do something else. I dart from class to class, getting assignment after assignment. I don't have time to even think about what I'm doing.

On the farm, we were taught to do things right, to do things thoroughly. I feel as though I'm just barely hanging on.

I put together a small filler article for the *Gazette*: favorite things of the seniors. These were some of the items:

> Favorite TV Show (drama): *Miami Vice*
> Favorite TV Show (comedy): *The Cosby Show and Cheers* (tie)

Favorite Movie: *Raiders of the Lost Ark*
Favorite Actors: Harrison Ford, Bill Murray
Favorite Singer: Bruce Springsteen
Favorite Song: "Born in the USA" ("Every Breath
    You Take" was a close second)
Favorite Athlete: Larry Bird (I had quite a few write-
    ins wishing that Bud Grant would return to
    coach the Vikings.)

It wasn't a great article. I wonder if I could write a really important article based around a survey—something of more lasting significance?

Thursday: I don't know how I get myself into these things! Well, I better start with right after school . . . .

Dad didn't have to work tonight so he and Mom went to Cherry Grove to see Amy in an afternoon volleyball game, then they decided to get groceries in Rochester.

For supper I ate leftovers alone. Amy came home halfway through my meal (such as it was), but she had already eaten on the way home—the bus had stopped at Hardee's.

In the evening, feeling rather lonely, I walked to the home volleyball game. Both A and B teams won. I must admit that I watched Melanie more than the game.

Afterwards I hung around talking to some of the guys. I kept hoping Melanie would come out of the locker room and I could talk to her.

Some of the last girls finally filtered out.

Sarah came up the stairs.

"Hi, Chad," she said. "You still here?" She had her dark hair tied back in a ponytail.

"Yeah. Just talking to the guys."

"Nice of you to come to the game."

I shrugged. "Well, I like to support the teams."

I started to walk toward the main doors. She followed.

"Good game," I said.

"Thanks."

"Everyone gone?" I glanced uncertainly back down the hall. I'm sorry to write that I was pretty obvious.

"Oh." She looked back. She caught on that I was waiting for someone else. "I was the last. A bunch of girls left the back way."

"Just wondering," I lied. "We can turn off some of the lights then."

"Sure."

"Leaving now?"

"Yeah. I was gonna call my dad." She laughed, a little embarrassed. "He likes to give me a ride, y'know, when it's dark." She jokingly pushed my arm, adding, "Even in Hillcrest."

"You can't be too careful. Dad always gives Amy a ride. But me," I shrugged, smiled, "I gotta walk."

She headed toward the hallway phone.

I felt I should suggest it, so I did: "I'll walk you home." I added, winking: "If you think it's safe."

"Oh," she said quickly, as if she hadn't thought of it before. "Okay. I'm sure Dad won't mind."

So, for the second time, I walked with Sarah. Maybe it was the cool fall night, the hint of winter, or just plain loneliness, but I asked her if she wanted to go with me to a Halloween party.

"Where at?" We passed under a streetlight and I could see her breath.

"Bob Swanson's house."

She frowned. "Mom and Dad will want to know if Bob's folks will be home."

I shrugged. "I guess they will be there. At least I would think so."

"Sometimes they're not." She stated it as if she knew.

"Oh."

"Well," she said brightly, "I'll check with my parents and let you know. How's that?"

"Okay," I said.

She grabbed my arm playfully, pulling herself close to me. "But I'll try to talk them into it."

"Okay," I said again.

I didn't know girls still checked with their parents for things like that. It wasn't like a big date or something. Then I realized that, in her eyes, maybe it was!

Friday: Another busy day.

I handed in my term paper on the Middle East. Last year I would've sweat blood over it but now it was easy. Mrs. W. was right—the more you write the easier it becomes.

Sarah saw me in the hall. She said that she could go to the party and to just let her know when to pick her up.

Oops. Forgot about the car! I made a mental note to check with Dad.

I talked to Aaron during lunch. He and Jennifer are going next week to the party. Sounds like the whole senior class is going—and a few juniors too, like Sarah.

This afternoon the team lost the football game over at West Concord. This evening we had play practice.

We're really getting down to the wire. Miss G. yelled at those still needing to use their scripts: "on book" she calls it. I was surprised when she started to chew those cast members out. I'd never seen her blow up. Then she launched into a speech about group responsibilities. I know if it had been me, I would've died right there.

As for my "role" in the play, she's having me practice with the lights. It's a pretty easy play for lights, she says.

"Do it right and no one will notice," she informed me. "Make one mistake and the whole town knows."

Great, I thought.

I must decide about the fall retreat. I don't want to go, but when Pastor Jim and your mom gang up on you, a guy doesn't stand a chance.

Saturday: A tiring day. Lots of yard work. Almost as good as being on the farm.

Sunday: Gave my $5 to Pastor Jim. Now I'm stuck for good.

Monday: End of quarter coming up on Friday. Four big tests this week—no time to write tonight.

Tuesday: Worked all hour in journalism with Melanie. We're writing an editorial on open enrollment, the concept that a student can pick his or her own school. I didn't know much about it before, but Melanie sure filled me in. I think it's a more significant issue in larger districts.

We've written together so often now that it's pretty easy to hit a pattern or style. We present the issue, then the pro's, then the con's, then a conclusion.

Melanie sat at the typewriter while I sat beside her. We composed it on the typewriter without a prior rough draft—a first for us. The words flowed from both of us and we really felt like professionals.

I also liked composing on a typewriter because I "had to" sit close enough so that I could read what Melanie typed. When we were finished, she pulled the sheet out with a flourish, leaned back, and handed the article to me.

Just as we finished (thinking highly of our quick techniques), Mrs. W. came by and reminded us that part of writing is rewriting.

As soon as Mrs. Webster moved on, Melanie turned to me: "Any typos?"

Our knees bumped. My pulse raced like a runaway horse.

"None that I see," I said.

"Good, because I need to work on my government term paper." She leaned close enough so that I felt her whispered breath on my cheek: "No matter what Mrs. Webster says."

"But your research paper was due Friday."

"I know." She crossed her arms. "But I got behind. It happens."

"Need any help?"

At first she shook her head, but then she smiled and her blue eyes sparkled. "I do need help filling it out—you know, fleshing out the words a bit. You're good with words."

I raised my eyebrows, trying to look suspicious. "You mean empty words?"

"It needs words." She smiled and winked. "Any kind."

So we spent the last part of the period (when we should've worked on the yearbook) on Melanie's term paper.

Maybe she likes me after all.

Wednesday: I got the car for Friday. I'll pick up Sarah at 7 p.m. We decided not to wear costumes. I'll admit that I wish I was taking Melanie. (or is that "were"? I hate verb tenses.)

Melanie was very friendly and sincerely appreciated my help yesterday. Another one of our editorials appeared in today's paper and we both heard many compliments.

Aaron jokingly calls me "Clark Kent" and Melanie "Lois Lane." I don't think he realizes the irony.

That's all tonight. Big tests tomorrow.

Thursday: Did just fine on the government test (I think) though the tests I feel most comfortable with I usually bomb and those I think I barely passed I often ace. I wonder why?

I showed Mrs. W. this journal today. Glancing at it, she was really impressed with how much I wrote. She gave me some extra credit, then added, "You didn't really need the points, but I'm glad you're writing."

Play practice is clicking now. All of the actors have their lines down, except Bob Swanson. He says he ad-libs his way through most plays. The rest of the cast is getting upset with him. True, he has a big part, but it seems to me that a big part means extra work. A person should be responsible.

It'll be interesting to go to his party tomorrow night. All I have ever been to are church parties (if you can call them that!) and school-sponsored class parties.

Friday: Home at last. I have to write and unwind. Both Mom and Dad were still awake when I got home. They didn't say anything, but I think they were a little surprised at the time. I hadn't watched the clock.

The evening started out on an awkward foot. I went to the door to get Sarah, and her dad answered—a big guy—must've played basketball and football. Wide face, bull neck, big hands, deep voice.

He shook my hand (almost crushed it) and asked me in.

"Sarah will be down in a minute."

I don't know why, but I started to really sweat—and I had put on extra deodorant!

He asked me how the school year was going.

"Fine," I said.

"Have a seat," he said. I sat down.

He answered the door for some trick or treaters. A moment later he returned and asked me what classes I enjoyed.

"None," I said, then grinned, trying to make a joke: "except journalism, of course."

A corner of his mouth lifted. "Of course."

Was that his laugh? If so, he could get a job with the Mafia.

Mrs. Webster bustled in from the kitchen. I know now how the trapped wagon train feels when the cavalry's bugle blows.

"Hi, Chad," she said. "I was just correcting some papers."

"Hi, Mrs. Webster." I thought about making some funny comment about my grade but decided I'd already pushed my luck to the breaking point.

None too soon, Sarah dashed down the stairs and grabbed her coat.

"When should we expect you?" Mrs. W. asked.

"Oh, about 12?" Sarah glanced at me, looking for confirmation. I didn't know what to say. I hadn't thought about it. I blushed, realizing that I should have.

"That's about right," I said quickly.

Her dad didn't looked pleased, but then maybe he never did.

"Not a minute past," I added.

Her dad nodded.

We got to Bob Swanson's at the right time, not the first or the last. He lived in the country, not too far from our old place. In fact it's a similar-looking big, old white farmhouse, but fixed up a lot more. Bob's family doesn't farm. When his parents moved to Hillcrest years ago, they bought just the house. I think his dad works at IBM in Rochester.

Cars packed the driveway. I parked along the roadside.

Again I noticed how pretty Sarah is—dark hair, nice figure, brown eyes. Yet, even though I was with one of the prettiest juniors, I still wished I was with Melanie. Maybe she'll be coming soon, I caught myself thinking.

The door opened. Bob, his dark hair slicked back, stood in the doorway in a black and red Dracula costume. "Come right in," he muttered in a poor Transylvanian accent. He smiled broadly, showing his fake vampire teeth. "Head to the left and drop your jackets, then go downstairs. My (he emphasized, raising his eyebrows) parents are getting the food ready."

In the basement they had several large rooms, one with a pool table, another with a sofa, big cushions, and a TV, and a third room with a Ping-Pong table. A fourth, smaller room was off to the side of the steps. It looked like an extra bedroom.

A Halloween movie was showing on the VCR.

Three guys were shooting pool while several girls watched.

No one was playing Ping-Pong in the adjoining room. I had always played Ping-Pong at junior high camp and thought I was pretty good. I asked if Sarah wanted to play.

She smiled. "Sure."

I soon discovered that she was better than I. After my second loss, I started getting flustered. Spectators had gathered.

I tried to joke around. My wisecracks fell flat. So did my volleys. I was feeling really warm.

Midway through the game Sarah missed several returns in a row. She didn't make it obvious, but the thought struck me that she wanted to make the game close. At that point, I was relieved. I didn't care how I saved face.

On a serve with English, I won the game. I wiped my forehead. It had been a workout.

Later I leaned close to her and whispered, "Did you let me win?" She smiled back. "No, I didn't let you win."

"Good."

But we both knew that she had let me catch up.

We watched a little of the movie, a horror-slasher film which neither of us cared for. Around 10 o'clock, Melanie showed up with Jay. Up close I didn't think he was so good-looking. In fact, with his long nose and chin, he was rather homely.

I talked to her a bit while Sarah was chatting with some other girls. Melanie introduced me to Jay.

He was amiable but was constantly looking elsewhere, scanning the crowd, obviously not interested in talking to me.

Later, Melanie saw me with Sarah. She looked a little surprised—maybe jealous? (At least that's my wishful thinking.)

Aaron and Jennifer came about 10:30. She was hanging on him as usual, almost as if she were afraid that if she let go he'd fly away like a freed helium balloon. She was cordial, almost friendly. In fact, as the evening went on I realized that she was so friendly I wondered if something was wrong.

Sarah and I left about 11:45, thanking Bob and his parents. By this time, Bob seemed a little strained but still outwardly cheerful.

Driving back to town, we started talking about ourselves, our families, our churches, everything. Thinking back, I realize now that I had done most of the talking.

I pulled up outside her home. We continued talking. She asked about my beliefs.

"I'm not sure," I said. "I know what my parents believe . . . what my mom believes . . . but I don't know if life is that simple."

Sarah didn't reply but nodded a lot.

Anyway, though rumors may fly in school on Monday about the car parked outside her home, let this record show that we just talked.

I finally walked her to her door. Only then did I realize the time: 1:OO a.m.!

I'm glad her dad didn't open the door.

I'll have to call her in the morning and apologize. I can't afford to have Mrs. Webster mad at me. She's probably changing my grade right now.

Saturday: Miss Gunderson called this morning. She told me that last night Mark Cassil came to the junior high dance with some ninth graders and threw up in the bathroom.

"He was drunk," she said. "He'll be suspended from extra-curricular activities for two weeks. Will you take his part?"

I think my heart stopped. "But how can I do both?"

"You know it's a small part—on and off. You could do it easily, maybe even better. You know the blocking, the timing."

"I guess so," I muttered reluctantly.

"Thanks! I knew I could count on you."

After I hung up, I sat down. My knees were shaking. I sat by the desk a long time. Then I went to my room, found my script and started memorizing.

Later in the day I called Sarah. Of all people, her dad answered. His voice boomed over the receiver: "Websters."

"Uh." Instantly my mouth was dry. "I'm sorry I got Sarah home late last night. We were talking and lost track of time."

"This must be Chad. That's fine. She told us already."

"Oh."

"Do you want to talk to Sarah?"

"Uh, sure."

"I'll call her. Say, Chad, it's nice of you to call and explain."

"Uh, sure."

So Sarah and I talked a few minutes. "I hope you're not in trouble with your parents."

"No," she said. "They were a little upset, but they saw your car outside and knew where I was. But if I hadn't come in when I did, Dad was ready to come out and, uh, break us up."

She laughed a bit, clear and pleasant.

I laughed too, relieved. "You mean break me up!"

Her voice sparkled good-naturedly over the phone: "Maybe."

She's a nice girl, but somehow not Melanie.

Sunday: I went to Sunday school today. That makes two weeks in a row! Pastor Jim made a big deal of my attendance. It feels weird, not having gone since seventh grade or so. I suppose I haven't gone because I don't have any close friends in church. Steve Mifflin and Walter Nicols are the only other guys my age— the rest are girls. In seventh grade that was a hindrance, but now it's not so bad. The girls, however, do stick to themselves a lot. Even in church you can't escape cliques.

* * *

FIRST SEMESTER, SECOND QUARTER

Monday: During rehearsal tonight I made my debut as an actor. I have never been so terrified in my life. Even though the bright lights kept me from seeing Miss G. or the other cast members sitting in the audience, my legs shook the whole time I was on stage.

And being out there in front of everyone, pretending to be someone else, was really bizarre. When Bob screamed at me/my character, I knew it was Bob but his face moved so differently. It was Bob, yet it wasn't. I can't even explain it clearly, but it was the strangest experience.

I hope I won't be so nervous tomorrow.

Tuesday: Long practice tonight because tomorrow's play-off football game eliminates tomorrow's practice. Too tired to write . . . .

Wednesday: Grades today. Best ones in my life. All B's with A's in journalism and building trades.

The football team lost its play-off game. Actually, I'm glad. It'll mean less stuff going on so I can concentrate on the play. Hopefully, Steve Mifflin can now really get into the part because he won't have to worry about football. I think, in some ways, he's like me. He holds lots of things inside.

Thursday: Tonight we went through the entire play. I was so nervous about my entrance that I forgot to cue the phone. Bob

Swanson had to ad-lib until I hit the sound effect. (Actually, to be honest, what happened was that Steve tapped my back, and then I remembered!)

Later, Bob chewed me out, but I think he really enjoyed showing off his ad-libbing skills. I wonder if he'll be a professional actor someday?

Practice went so well (except for my goof) that Miss G. canceled rehearsal tomorrow. Everyone, she explained, could use a night off before the final countdown.

At that moment I realized that I had forgotten to tell Miss G. that I was leaving after school tomorrow for a church retreat and would miss rehearsal. Fortunately, since there would be no practice, I was saved from having to explain at this late date why I couldn't be there!

Sunday: We just got home from the church retreat a little bit ago. My mind is swimming. I better write now while the memories are clear.

Friday we climbed into two cars parked outside the church and threw our clothes and sleeping bags into the trunks. The girls went in the LTD with Chris, Pastor Jim's wife. Walter Nicols, Steve Mifflin, and I piled into Pastor Jim's Nova.

"I'm really glad all three of you could make it," Pastor Jim said as we drove out of town.

"Miss Gunderson said it was okay a couple of weeks ago," Steve explained.

I didn't mention that I had forgotten to even ask.

"She seems like a good teacher."

We were heading southeast, toward the Mississippi.

"She is," said Steve. "She talked me into going out for this play."

"Me too," I piped in. This was the most I had heard Steve talk—except for memorized lines—in my life.

"How about you?" Pastor Jim glanced at Walter. "How's school?"

"Fine," he said cheerfully. Walter, wide-faced, dark-haired, short but really strong, isn't too bright. Kids accept him because in football he's dependable on the line and in track he's great in the shot put, but that's as far as it goes. Kids are pretty fickle.

I gazed out the window. Southeastern Minnesota is fascinating. The roads wind between rocky bluffs and down into steep-sided valleys. We passed tiny farms hidden down in the valley basins. Small cornfields follow the shape of fast-flowing streams. We passed old railroad lines and trestles and drove through towns even smaller than Oak Center.

Once we got to the camp overlooking the Mississippi, we unloaded the cars. For supper we cooked hot dogs over a fire that we built in a stone fire ring.

Since the girls kept to themselves, Steve, Walter and I got to know each other pretty well. Steve and Walter, I discovered, had been doing things together for years. Both don't have many outside friends. Though Steve is generally well liked, he's so quiet that other kids don't get close to him. Also, he's never been a member of the party set, something most people have to do to be popular. As for Walter, well, he doesn't fit in easily with most people.

Saturday morning, while the girls went hiking, Pastor Jim and the three of us went trout fishing in the creek that runs into the Mississippi. Pastor Jim and Steve had fly rods and wore vests and generally looked like something out of a fishing catalogue. Walter and I had old fishing poles. We spread out through the high grass along the edge of Clearwater Creek. I could hear Pastor Jim and Steve nearby and the clicking of their fly reels. Walter and I sat back on the stream bank and dropped in our worms.

It was a scenic, peaceful valley—tall oaks and maples, the cold rippling creek, the dry fall air.

Walter shouted: "I've got a big one!"

I dashed through the tall grass to his spot. He was so excited he slipped down the steep bank and fell into the water. By this time Pastor Jim was there too. He leaped in after Walter, water gushing over his hip boots, and helped him up. Walter spit out water and shook his head free of water but still gripped his rod.

His fish was bending the rod in half! The fish shot downstream, the drag screaming. Pastor Jim held the rod along with Walter and both were laughing at the size of the fish. Steve stood on the bank behind me, watching too. Pastor Jim adjusted the drag on Walter's reel and let go and Walter was finally able to reel it in.

Then we all laughed, for it was the biggest sucker any of us had ever seen.

We brought it back and took a picture of it before we killed it. Even though we all poked fun at Walter for catching a sucker, I was a little envious. Even a sucker was better than what the rest of us caught—nothing.

Before lunch we had a Bible study and a testimony time. Pastor Jim and Chris seem to have a really good marriage. They joked with each other, shared their deepest feelings, and didn't seem to hide behind masks. I wonder if I'll ever have a marriage like that?

Anyway, the group sat by the lodge's fireplace and talked about different things, mostly their frustrations with school and conflicts with friends. I didn't feel comfortable talking, so I just listened.

That afternoon, after a long volleyball game, Pastor Jim and I went fishing again while Steve and Walter napped. He seemed quite interested in my future plans, more so, in fact, than in fishing.

"I don't know what I'll do," I said. "I always planned to take some agriculture classes, then farm with my dad. But now I'll probably go to vo-tech. Maybe I could handle college."

"How's your relationship with God?" he asked.

I knew what he was getting at. I had made a decision for Christ in the fifth grade, but I didn't know then—not really—what I was doing . . . or "deciding."

"Sure, I've prayed about it," I said.

"Have you really committed your future to the Lord?"

We got to what looked like a good fishing hole and I worked my worm onto the hook. It squirmed a lot, like me. "I guess," I answered.

I flipped my worm into the stream. He pulled out some fly line and cast downstream of me. He didn't say anything for awhile. I was relieved.

"Don't expect a telegram from heaven," he said. "The

beginning point is your relationship with God. The rest follows. 'Commit your ways unto the Lord, trust also in Him and He will bring it to pass.'"

Neither of us caught anything that afternoon.

Saturday night we ate canned spaghetti and meatballs, played volleyball under the lights, and sang songs before bed.

Sunday we had a special service of singing and Bible study.

All of us tried fishing that afternoon. Two of the girls caught several nice trout. Can you figure it?

On the drive back home, we were all exhausted. You'd think a retreat should have rejuvenated us.

"We're relaxed," Pastor Jim explained.

Thinking back on the weekend, I'm confused. Everyone talked about commitment and complete surrendering to the Lord. Even Walter shared how God's worked in his life. I don't know. I'm not ready for it, I guess.

Mom is sure of her salvation.

Maybe I'm not sure I want to be sure. I know there are many different viewpoints in life—I can see that even as I write editorials for the paper.

Oh well, time will tell.

Monday: This morning Dad and Mom were snapping at each other again. There must have been a fight. Whenever they have a big argument, they are curt and impatient and edgy for days. I was glad that I hadn't been home this past weekend. Later, I pieced together that they had argued about me.

On the way to school, Dad asked if I had had a good weekend. From his tone of voice, I guessed that he hoped I hadn't.

"It was okay," I said.

"But it wasn't great?"

"We had some fun—played games, went fishing, hiked nice trails. I got to know Steve and Walter and the others better."

"But it wasn't great?" he repeated. Those must've been my mother's words and he was sure I had hated the retreat.

I tried to walk the middle ground. I didn't want to get into the middle of a fight on a Monday morning. "Not the greatest," I replied, "but I'm glad I went."

He drove into the school parking lot. His scowl and set jaw told me that he wasn't happy, but at least he wasn't angry.

As we got out of the car, I shifted my schoolbooks and said, "If you didn't want me to go, you should've said so. I wouldn't have."

He glanced at me, really startled. He stammered a bit. "It, well, it's not that. I just didn't think you'd enjoy it. Your mother was sure you would."

"Oh."

Let him stew on it, I thought. Maybe he'll realize my going wasn't worth arguing about. A person has to be honest. That's what he always says. Honest, even with himself.

Once at school, I settled into a chair in the commons and finished my homework. Steve and Walter joined me shortly before the first bell.

We acted a little awkwardly with each other. Before the weekend, we rarely talked, but now we shared a deeper friendship. That friendship worked on the retreat, but would it work at school? I really appreciate Steve and Walter. They are both genuine. They may hide their deepest feelings, but they don't put on masks to fool others. I hope our friendship works.

In the evening, though, Steve had to hide his "nice guy" self and wear the mask of the insane killer, Jonathan. He doesn't appear nervous, yet he is always so reserved that he rarely shows any stress.

On a sudden impulse, I asked Miss G. if I could see if Walter would help me with the lights. After a momentary hesitation, she said it was a good idea.

I called him after practice. He didn't jump at it right away and I thought that maybe he didn't want to, but the more we talked about it, I remembered that I didn't jump at the chance either. Somehow I knew Walter was thrilled. He just couldn't let on.

Tuesday: Miss G. saw me in the hall, said I was doing a good job but that I needed to put myself more into the part of Gibbs. I don't understand. If I were Gibbs, I never would act as stupidly as he does. This acting is not for me.

At supper, Amy told my parents about me being in the play. I had wanted to keep it a surprise.

Dad stared at me for a second, I think in shock. His eyebrows twitched. Mom wiped her apron and congratulated me.

"How did this come about?" Dad asked. Maybe he was impressed, maybe not. With him it's hard to tell.

So I told them.

"I'll call Sheila today," Mom beamed. "They'll want to come."

"Mom, not the relatives!" I moaned.

Amy was grinning like a cat with a trapped mouse—me.

"They'll be hurt if they found out afterwards," Dad decreed. I was doomed as soon as Dad assumed the somber voice of authority. "We better tell Grandpa too."

Dead meat.

Wednesday: No more typewriters. At least that's what I envision. Today Mrs. W. got twelve computers for the journalism class and several printers. From now on, all final articles are to be typed on the Apple IIe's. She said larger schools use them all the time. We save our articles on the floppy disks. It's amazing how we can write with them. We can revise articles easily. No more correcting-type. No more cut and pasting. No more rewriting a whole page because the last line was botched.

When I got home, I found out that Aunt Sheila's bringing the five cousins and Grandpa over for the play. Uncle Bob can't make it. I should be glad for small favors.

I'll be shaking all over. Maybe I won't survive.

Better study now for Thursday's tests. I'm gonna be a wreck. I'll probably dream about the Titanic.

Thursday: Aaron came early to school today and sat with me in the commons. He was acting really weird, like something was bothering him, really bad, so bad that he couldn't talk about it. When Steve and Walter joined us, he acted even more uncomfortable.

He left before the first bell, probably to find Jennifer. "Talk to you later," he mumbled.

I wonder if he's sick.

I've been so busy with the play I haven't had time to talk to him. I know I've written in this journal before about Aaron. Most of the things we used to do together were in school, but summers I'd sometimes ride my bike over to his farm and we'd take off for Vulture Valley, explore the caves and hike down to the river.

Life changes so quickly.

So unexpectedly.

Two years ago I never would've dreamed we'd be off the farm. Or I'd be in the play. Or write articles for the paper. Or keep a journal.

Friday: Talked to Sarah today. She was friendly but a little strained. She seemed angry with me for some reason.

I told her I'd been out of town on a church retreat. She perked up and asked all sorts of questions. I hope she's not getting any serious ideas.

I think I'm finally getting the hang of this acting. As Miss G. says, you've gotta make a fool out of yourself so you won't look foolish. Throw yourself into the part and really ham it up, then you'll look good.

Unfortunately, by the time I quit shaking, I'm off stage. No matter how nervous I get, though, the light cues will go fine—they're too simple to foul up. But what about the sound effects?

Walter sits behind me, following the book. That should

reassure me, but he gets lost so easily. Well, as Miss G. says, plays are a good experience. No matter what happens, I know that the audience will laugh. But will I?

I wonder what Walter's going to do after school? Does he ever worry about his future?

Saturday: Dad and I put up storm windows and caulked around the siding. Whatever problems existed between Mom and Dad seem patched up again.

I'm sure it boils down to leaving the farm. For me, my future expectations vanished. For Dad, his past accomplishments were ripped away—as well as his future dreams. I know that has to be hard, but how long do you hang onto the past?

In school they tell us to expect many career changes. I'm glad I took journalism. Being able to write will help in just about any field.

This evening I called Aaron to see if he wanted to go to Rochester. He was just leaving to go over to Jennifer's and didn't have time to talk. He still sounded weird. You know how someone just doesn't seem himself?

I called Steve to see if he wanted to get a pizza or something. He couldn't. His family was having a big get-together and he was expected to hang around.

I almost called Sarah but didn't.

It was quiet evening. I watched TV. Nothing good was on, but I watched anyway.

Monday: Big dress rehearsal tonight. It went well but I'm as tired as if I'd walked beans all day in the hot sun.

The costumes ignited everyone's acting. Steve looked terrific—or should I say ugly? Miss G. sprayed his blond hair black and darkened his eyes. He didn't say anything at the time, just grinned in his quiet way.

She grayed my hair and drew on some wrinkles. At the last

minute, I decided to back into the sofa when I'm running away from Mortimer. I did a back somersault over the sofa and landed on my feet, then ran out.

Bob Swanson stared for a second or two, then he went on with his lines. Vicky and Sally, the two old ladies, giggled a bit out of character but quickly recovered. Miss G. nearly died laughing. Evidently the somersault was okay.

It's late. Better try to get to sleep.

(Because of the music concert tomorrow night, we won't be able to practice. I'll be able to catch up on my sleep!)

Tuesday: An interesting day.

I worked with Melanie on the word processor. Whenever I'm with her I feel different, excited. She always has the right amount of makeup, the right perfume, the right clothes, and her hair is always fixed just right.

When we began work on our editorial, she was a little "owly" as Mom calls it. Melanie seemed angry at the world. Normally I take the "con" position in our articles, but this time she wanted to take it. Oh well, who can figure girls?

As we finished I said, "You sure look nice today." She wore a dress because of the conference music concert at Cherry Grove. Her dress, a deep red velvet, shaped her figure nicely.

"Are you coming to the music festival tonight?"

Before that second I hadn't planned on it.

"Maybe," I replied slowly, my mind spinning along the maze of possibilities. "Thought I'd see, uh, about my homework."

"It'll be very good," she smiled, pressing the print key and turning to me. "Though if you come, don't listen to my solo closely. I'm stretching for those high notes."

"I'm afraid I wouldn't know what to listen for. I'm not very musical."

"Well, come anyway. It'll be good."

That was that. I was instantly a music fan.

Dad let me have the car. No one else wanted to go, so I went alone, which was fine with me. Once there, I sat near the front. I figured if I was going to listen to the conference choir, Melanie had better see me.

As she filed in with the rest of the choir, she spotted me and winked in my direction. Her shining hair shaped her high cheekbones.

A few songs were good but most were too classical for my tastes. I like a song with a strong rhythm. Her solo, though, was fantastic. I sure couldn't tell anything was too high for her. The crowd gave her a good ovation and she beamed brightly and bowed gracefully.

After the concert, people were milling around. I walked over to Melanie and congratulated her on the solo.

"Thanks." She smiled warmly, grabbing my arm and squeezing it. "Thanks for coming."

A lot of people filtered past us, many complimenting her. She was in her glory, like at homecoming. This time, though, I was standing by her. And I was hoping Jay wouldn't show up.

"Let's go get a drink of water," she said.

The crowd was thinning. School busses and vans began to load. In the hall, after a drink, she turned to me, stood close. "I hear you're in the play now."

"Yeah." I shrugged and looked off down the mostly empty hallway. "Just a fill in. My real job is stage manager."

"Everything's important, you know. I hope to be in the spring musical again this year."

"I'm sure you'll make it," I said.

"Maybe you'll be there too." She smiled again, giving my arm a parting squeeze. "The school van's loading. See you tomorrow."

"Sure," I said.

She buttoned her coat and ran off, then glanced back at me and waved. I smiled at her and waved back.

On my drive home, I wondered where her family had been.

Wednesday: The paper came out today with a picture of the cast (with me) and my by-lined article on the front page.

"You running this paper?" Aaron joked at lunch, opening his milk carton.

"In a few years he'll be running the town paper," Steve added, sitting down beside me.

"He'll probably be chief editor of the *Minneapolis Tribune!*" topped Aaron. "Who was that famous newspaper guy—you know, 'Go west, young man'?"

Puzzled, we all shrugged.

"Good trivia question," Steve announced. "We all read it in tenth grade. For two cents and a free trip to Oak Center—"

Walter swallowed some milk, waited for a round of silence: "Horace Greeley."

Aaron nearly spit out his instant mashed potatoes. "That's it! Chad Horace Greeley Wilson!"

I'm afraid a new nickname was born at that moment. The rest of the day, I was known as Horace . . . . even at final dress rehearsal.

Thursday: Pastor Jim called after school. "Break a leg," he said.

"Huh?"

"That's what you say in the theater, isn't it?"

"Oh. I guess so. I'm new at this."

Later I discovered that he was right. After everyone was ready, Miss Gunderson, wearing a silky blue dress, gave her final instructions, then said "Break a leg."

"Why do they say that?" I asked Bob as we checked over our costumes.

"It's bad luck to say 'good luck' in the theater."

Seemed goofy logic to me.

We went behind the main curtain. I set the lights, dimmed the backstage. They opened the gym doors. Several young kids ran to the front seats. I paced backstage along with Sally and Vicky. Their gray hair and wrinkles looked authentic. I peeked at the audience through the curtain.

"Hey, bad luck to do that," Bob teased, tapping my shoulder. He didn't seem nervous at all.

My hands were perspiring, my feet cold.

The house was about two-thirds full, about 200 people.

"Good Thursday crowd," Miss G. said, coming backstage. "Five minutes everyone! Chad, watch the clock and flick the house lights in four minutes. In five, kill them."

I sat behind the light panel, nervously adjusting my chair. Walter stood behind me with a flashlight ready.

We hit the lights, began the play.

Midway through Act I came my cue to enter. As it approached, my nervousness increased, my heart pounding like a sledgehammer.

"Time to go," Walter whispered.

I got up, wiped my sweaty hands on my pants, and quickly crossed behind the set in order to reach the other side of the stage.

The scene with me flew by so quickly it seemed that it was over before it had even begun. Walter said I was great, but it was all a blur to me. I was only vaguely aware of my lines, the audience laughter, me falling over the sofa.

Everything went well. A good opening night. One down, two to go.

Friday: Writing in study hall:

Those who saw the play last night were impressed. Everyone raved about Bob S. (of course), but I also heard lots of good comments about Steve, Vicky and Sally.

Before school Sarah came by "our table" in the commons and congratulated me on a good debut. Walter was there, but Steve must've slept in. Aaron hadn't shown up yet.

She glanced at the empty chairs.

"Join us?" I asked.

"Sure." She sat down across from me. "So, do you think it will go well tonight?"

"Of course," I replied with great bravado, leaning back in my chair. "I'm the stage manager, you know, the guy in charge. Right, Walter?"

"Whatever you say," he muttered as he hunched over his math book.

"What are you up to now that volleyball's over?" I asked.

"Just getting caught up with classes. Mom and Dad insist I keep my grades up . . . or else."

"She's a teacher, after all."

"So's my dad—or was. He was phy-ed teacher and football coach over at Spring Meadow until it consolidated."

"What's he do now?"

"Works at IBM. He wanted to stay in teaching, but schools won't hire someone with a lot of experience."

"I guess other people lose their careers too, like us losing the farm."

She ran a hand over her brown hair. "We went through it when I was in the fourth grade. Because Mom had only taught a few years before I was born, she was able to get her job here—" Her voice trailed off and she shrugged.

Melanie was strolling our way. She wore a loose green blouse and nicely fitting slacks. I stared at her a moment, then glanced back to Sarah. Her brown eyes were studying me closely.

"You should've told me about your parents the other day," I said, feeling rather sheepish. "You let me babble on and on about our troubles."

"It was good to hear about someone else going through similar things, if you know what I mean. Besides, it was getting too late to go into our past trials. It's all behind us now."

Walter had been politely ignoring us, struggling with his math. On the word "late," his curiosity snapped into high gear. Melanie walked up to me, laid her hand on my shoulder.

"Chad," she said brightly, "good performance last night."

"Thanks," I said. I think I blushed. "Want to join us?"

She glanced at Sarah. "No, I've gotta run. See you later."

She was gone, leaving only the faint lingering scent of her perfume.

Aaron ambled over. "Seen Jen yet? I was supposed to pick her up, but she was gone by the time I got to her house."

The first bell rang and we were off to our classes. I wonder where all these morning meetings are heading. I get less homework done each day!

—Added journal entry, 11 P.M.—

The performance tonight was even better. Everyone was more relaxed, yet still nervous enough to provide enough energy.

I almost missed my first telephone cue but Walter tapped me. I had been intent on watching Bob and Jo in the Elaine scene. Other than that near disaster, a flawless evening.

Two down, one to go.

Saturday: Good news and bad.

First the bad. Afternoon pandemonium. Dad picked up grandpa from the nursing home and brought him over. My aunt and cousins came over too. The rug rat cousins drove me crazy. I cannot tolerate undisciplined and hyper little kids. Aunt Sheila herself acted really hassled from wrestling with those five kids. And then Grandpa talked non-stop. He doesn't hear well, but he sure chatters once you get him started! Mom, usually the stabilizing influence in our family, flitted nervously from one food preparation to another. Dad didn't help at all, well, he did sit awhile with Grandpa.

Of course, I can't point a finger at anyone else's hyper state when I was a nervous wreck the whole day. I kept wondering what the cousins would do during the play to embarrass me.

When evening came, my stomach felt like it was knotted up by an entire Boy Scout troop.

When the play began, I thought I was going to throw up.

I hit all the sound and light cues correctly in the first scene, but a short time later I nearly wrecked the whole play. As I made my way around the set for my entrance, I nearly tripped over a stage brace. I had visions of the set falling down and the audience seeing me standing behind the wreckage!

I heard my cue, entered, and spewed out my first line (too quick! I told myself).

Mortimer (Bob) was on the "phone" as usual. The ladies ushered me to the table, offered wine. Again, as usual.

I smiled at them—so far, so good—and then I looked them right in the eyes.

My mind went completely blank. There I was—Chad Wilson—on stage, family in the second row, and all I could think of was "What am I doing in front of all these people?"

Bob came in with his line. He delivered it big so he got a good laugh, but his inflection wasn't quite the same. Either that, or he had reworded his line a little. All I know is that panic exploded in my head like a nuclear war. What was my line? My tongue felt swollen and I couldn't catch my breath.

And so I sat between two "old ladies" with Mortimer leaning over me and my memory totally obliterated and I couldn't think of anything to say.

I grabbed the glass again, lifted it, and struggled to remember my line.

Then Vicky—I could've kissed her!—covered for me by making up a line. At the same time, Sally whispered my line to me.

Saved!

We continued. I did my falling bit and ran off stage, none too soon! During intermission the three actors chewed me out. As soon as they saw that I felt bad, we all laughed about it. After all, we did make it through the scene. Miss G. didn't say anything except, "A little pause there."

No one else (except Walter) seemed to notice.

Now the good news.

The cast party at Miss G.'s apartment was great. She had all sorts of games set up. Mr. Monroe (he's single—I wonder if there's anything between them?) helped her with the serving.

Everyone had a good time. A few people (Bob S. and the cops in the play) left pretty early, but the rest stayed until midnight.

Miss G. thanked all of us. We presented her with a gift certificate then watched Friday's performance on her VCR. (I wonder if we'll get one soon? Most people seem to have them now.)

It was a lot of fun, but I don't think I'll ever be in a play again—too much stress!

Sunday: Mom and Dad both went to church today. In fact they dragged me out of bed to go. At least they let me sleep through Sunday school.

I'm not sure why Dad decided to go. He hasn't gone since I was in grade school.

During announcements Pastor Jim mentioned Steve, Walter, and me and our contribution to the school play.

Several people came up after church and congratulated us, said how thoroughly they enjoyed it, hadn't laughed so much in years, etc.

I wonder . . . is that why Dad decided to go to church?

Monday: I couldn't believe how sad it was after school when we struck the set. We ripped off the Dutchman, took down the flats, dismantled the scaffolding, and pried off my railing. I can still hear Teddy (Jason) shouting "Charge!" up San Juan Hill. We swept the stage afterwards and pulled the curtains back. The flats are now all stored in the wings.

The plain wood stage now stands bare, overlooked by the lime-green brick walls. No sign that a play had ever taken place is left, no evidence that for eight weeks we had worked together, learned together, laughed together.

Miss G. said that she always felt sad striking the set. So much work goes into it and just when the production gets good, we take it down.

Even as we were working, basketball players were in the gym shooting buckets.

Life goes on.

Tuesday: Lots of studying. Tests tomorrow.

Wednesday: Went to the church's Thanksgiving Banquet tonight. All of us "young people" (I hate that term) served the adults and then ate. The guest speaker was pretty good—he kept changing his pitch and tempo, things I had learned about through the play, and that made him more interesting to listen to.

His topic was commitment and he really made me think. What are my values? Do I have any real commitments? I wonder if the values my parents hold are for me? Even though Dad rarely goes to church, I think he still believes in Biblical commandments. I want to find out for myself what is right before I commit myself to anything.

If Pastor Jim ever asks me again about where I'm going with my life, I think I'll tell him that I don't know, but I'm thinking. When I make commitments, they will be informed ones. They will be real.

Maybe each person has to figure these things out for himself. When I'm old I don't want to find out that I asked the wrong questions and never got the right answers.

Thanksgiving Weekend: Nothing special. Got together with the relatives. Grandpa wasn't feeling very well today, seemed kind of down.

I remember one Thanksgiving when we went to Wisconsin to visit some of Mom's relatives. It was really fun because I met four cousins on that side of the family who were my age.

How do I sum up the day? Lots of food. Lots of TV football. Rest.

Sunday Night: Vacations sure go fast.

Monday: Everyone seemed tired. Dad was sleepy this morning as he drove to school, and Steve and Walter said little in the commons, and I kept yawning.

In building trades everyone moved slowly shingling the roof even though it was cold outside. Moving quickly was the only way to stay warm. (Now that I think about it, Mr. Jameson and I are the only hustlers in the group.) In journalism everyone just picked at the fall yearbook material as if it were food that no one really wanted to eat

Is everyone waiting for Christmas?

Late in the day I talked to Aaron. Since Jennifer's cheering tomorrow and needs to be at school before the game to practice, Aaron offered to give me a ride to the game. Maybe it'll be a chance to find out what's eating him. Melanie's a winter cheerleader too—I wonder, is a double date ever possible? How serious is she with this Jay-bird?

Tuesday: What an evening! Boys and girls A squad double-header. Girls won but not an exciting game. I just don't think they're as exciting to watch as the boys. The ball doesn't move as fast around the court. Does that mean I'm a chauvinist? (Mrs. W. is encouraging us to use bigger words.)

Anyway, Aaron was in a good mood, practically his old light-hearted self. He laughed, he joked, he was loud, he was obnoxious. However, when we sat on the bleachers and the cheerleaders came out, he quieted down.

No one was sitting near us so I asked him if he was feeling okay.

"Yeah," he said. "It's just Jennifer. I don't know about us."

Long pause.

The players were introduced over the loud speaker.

"What do you mean?"

"She wants to be the first senior with a ring. You know, to get married."

"Oh."

"I've always wanted to finish college and get my business going before settling down."

"You've always said that." The ref blew the opening whistle. The centers jumped. The ball went our way. "She won't wait?"

"I don't think she really wants more school. She could get a job and help me pay for school, but I don't know if I want that."

I never thought I'd hear Aaron confused or doubting himself. I couldn't say anything. What kind of advice could I give?

I wondered, though, if Jennifer was afraid of the future. Was she afraid of losing Aaron after graduation? Several of the hot romances between last year's seniors ended during the summer. At the time I thought it was odd, but maybe it's a common thing. Maybe high school romances, like high school friends, remain in high school.

Sarah played a little during the game. She moved quickly and smoothly but she's better in VB than in basketball. I must admit, though, that I watched Melanie a lot more. I think she noticed my attention.

I wanted to hang around after the game because Melanie didn't have Jay waiting, but Aaron wanted to leave right away. He didn't want to talk to Jennifer.

What'll happen to them?

Wednesday: This morning in the commons I waved Sarah over to our table. I told her she played a good game.

She sat across from me, next to Steve. "I like volleyball better."

"You gotta like what you do," said Steve, not looking up from his homework, "otherwise you won't do well."

Everyone turned to Steve, shocked that he would speak if not spoken to. He blushed a bit at the sudden attention. He stammered: "That's what the coach always says in football."

"Thanks, coach," Sarah smiled.

The rest of the day, we called him "Coach Mifflin."

Mrs. Webster assigned me another article, covering (what else?) the next play—a one act. I didn't even know Hillcrest High put one on!

Come to think of it, though, I did hear Bob and Jason discussing "last year's one-act" at the cast party.

I better not get roped into this one. This quarter I have another government term paper and I haven't even picked a topic!

Thursday: In the morning I saw Miss G. She gave me info on the one-act. Try-outs in two weeks, right before Christmas vacation. Practice starts in January. I'll write a short article and follow with a bigger one in two weeks.

She also asked if I wanted to go on the field trip to the Guthrie Theater in Minneapolis. The trip was primarily for her play production class but was open to anyone in the fall play.

I said I'd think about it and she asked if I'd check with Walter. He was welcome to come too.

It might be kind of fun.

Snow's in the forecast. We're late with it this year. I miss snowmobiling across our fields. Our snowmobiles were sold, along with everything else.

Friday: Aaron and I went to the girls' home game tonight—no boys' game today. Amy tagged along for the ride but, once at school, she ran off to the seventh grade corner of the bleachers. We sat near the center—best view of the court, best view of the cheerleaders.

"How are things between you and Jennifer?" I ventured.

"About the same," Aaron said. "I've been thinking we should break up for awhile, maybe date others." He shrugged.

I knew she wouldn't appreciate that idea.

Steve and Walter came and sat by us. That ended Aaron's conversation.

Aaron is always friendly to them but distant. Maybe he sees them as not fitting in. They're strong churchgoers, and they don't go to the parties. But for that matter, neither do I. What would it be like to be one of the elite, one who goes everywhere, who's always invited? Even if I had stayed in FFA, even been FFA president, I don't think I'd have ever been one of the chosen few.

The girls lost. Sarah played more once the verdict was in. As always, coaches give the "scrubs" experience once the game is lost.

Melanie looked as great as ever. This time a guy with a Pine Crest letter jacket was with her. So much for my chance.

After the game, Aaron asked if I wanted to go to a party at Swanson's. We could drop Amy off and drive out there.

"Maybe," I said. I wondered if Melanie and her new boyfriend would be there.

"What about Jennifer?"

"I suppose we should pick her up," he said.

Without thinking I passed the invitation along to Steve and Walter. They glanced uncertainly at each other. Aaron kept looking over the gym but nudged my arm. Oops. Evidently it was a private invitation.

"Not this time," Steve said diplomatically. "But how about we all go to Rochester for pizza?"

Aaron declined at first, then, for some reason, reconsidered. He turned to Steve. "Why not?" he grinned.

I wonder if he was looking for a way to declare his independence from Jennifer?

I'm glad I'm not in a romantic bind like that. Aaron was a real clown at the pizza place—like he used to be.

By the way, the weathermen were wrong again. No snow.

Saturday: The entire family went Christmas shopping in Rochester. Dad took us out to eat and then we split up at the mall. I'm glad I still have some money saved from my summer jobs.

I didn't find anything but I came up with some ideas for everyone, everyone except Grandpa. What can I possibly get him?

Sunday: I went to Sunday school for the first time in a few weeks. Pastor Jim started a study on values. It looked interesting but I didn't want to commit myself to every Sunday, so I didn't take a study book with me.

Later, Dad and I put some plastic on the windows and did

some final fall pruning in the yard. Mom frowned at our working on Sunday, but it had to get done. Guess we were lucky the snow has held off.

Monday: Guthrie trip on Friday. My money and permission slip is in. Melanie's going too. Miss G. had an extra ticket and said she could go since she's been in quite a few musicals. It should be a lot of fun. I've only been to the Cities a couple of times in my life.

I decided to do my term paper on the government farm policies. I know I'll have to narrow it down, but at least I have something to start with. Maybe I should offer Melanie my help right away?

I'm going to call her . . .

Her mother answered—Melanie wasn't there. She didn't say when she'd be home. Mrs. Johnson took my message but she sounded tired. I was puzzled. It wasn't that late that she'd be going to bed yet. I hope I didn't make a bad impression.

I better talk to Mom and Dad about getting a job. If I could get a date with Melanie, I'd need some money. Christmas is going to deplete my meager extra savings. Mom and Dad insist I keep the bulk of my savings for college.

Tuesday: When I first saw Melanie she acted as if she hadn't heard my message. Later, we sat at the same table typing on different computers.

I was the most nervous I've ever been, far worse than during the play. Did she know I had called and was she giving me the cold shoulder? Or hadn't her mother delivered the message? My stomach hurt, it was knotted so tight. My lips felt dry as an old corncob.

Near the end of the period, she turned her printer on and said, "Say, Chad, my mom said you called last night."

I was shocked, but if she was going to be casual, so could I.

"Oh, yeah. I was working on my term paper and thought that maybe you'd like some help before the deadline."

She stared at her copy coming out of the printer. "Maybe," she finally said. "I haven't started yet. If I need help, I'll give you a call."

"Fine."

So much for that.

I've been depressed all day.

Wednesday: I decided this morning that if Melanie doesn't want to see more of me, so what? Life isn't finished. She's not worth getting depressed over.

Miss G. caught me in the hall and wanted to know if I was coming out for the one-act.

"I should get a job," I hedged.

"I never pressure anyone," she replied. "But you did so well in the last play, and I could use your help on this one."

I started to go.

"If you want to audition, the schedule is very flexible. We can work around almost anything, even a job."

I was flattered that she wanted me to audition . . . but it consumes all my time. I said I'd think about it.

Mom and Dad said a job would be okay. Tomorrow I'll check around town.

Thursday: I found a job at Hillcrest Pizza. I don't know much about it but they'll train me. Mr. Richter, the owner, knows Dad (everyone knows everyone else in Hillcrest) and said if I was as hard a worker and as honest as my father, I'd do all right.

I'll be trained next week so I can work over Christmas vacation. Maybe I could save enough for college AND a car?

Better get working on my term paper—I want to use vacation time to make money, not research the farm crisis. (Speaking of which: a few weeks ago Dad voted again for Ronald Reagan, along with just about everyone else, and will defend him with his last breath, yet the government's policies have been the cause of many family farms going under, including ours. The more I read about our government policies, the more the President seems to be a figurehead, like the Queen in England. The real power seems to lie with the bureaucrats and corporations. Hey, remember that for my conclusion!)

Friday: A great day! I think my mouth fell open so many times that birds could've nested there.

I'll record first things first.

The theater was great. We went on a backstage tour, met some actors (one was really weird, hair halfway down his back like a refugee from the sixties!), and one actor demonstrated putting on her makeup, and then a technician showed off their lights. I wish we had a tenth of their equipment.

The play was fantastic. Everyone was in character all the time and the costumes were great. Special effects—when Marley's ghost came up out of the floor with all the green lights and smoke, I nearly jumped out of my seat. The play was full of Christmas carols and dynamic dancing. I could sit through that play ten times and not see everything.

But the day wasn't over. On the bus ride home, Melanie sat in the seat in front of me. As we rode into Hillcrest, she turned around, smiled.

"Chad, if your offer is still good to help me with my paper, why don't you come over Sunday afternoon?"

I think I'm in heaven.

Saturday: Snow flurries in the morning and I worked all day on my paper. The rough draft is done and it's still three weeks before the end of the quarter (almost five when you count vacation!) This must be a school record!

Sunday: My head is swimming! Better put everything in order . . . .

Cold day. Little bit more snow, about two inches accumulated. Tried to sleep in but Mom woke me for Sunday school. Missed the first ten minutes. Class discussed drinking. What's there to know? Lots of drunk drivers in this world.

Kids were pretty open. I was surprised. They talked about the abundance of drinking—drugs too.

I didn't realize use and abuse was so common. I've always assumed that drugs were available, but the farm kept me so busy I never had time or opportunity or inclination to go looking for either drugs or alcohol.

During church all I could think of was Melanie.

At 3 o'clock I drove over to her house on the edge of town. It's a small one and a half-story house with faded green aluminum siding. The windows needed paint and so did the garage.

I walked up to the aluminum storm door. The doorbell button was cracked. I knocked.

Melanie opened the inner wooden door. Her hair was neatly pulled back and she wore a big pink sweater and jeans. She smiled warmly and opened the storm door.

She noticed my notebook and pen. "Good. You came prepared."

She led me through a small entryway, past a darkened room on the right to a small room off the dining room. A typewriter sat on a small oak table, surrounded by lots of books.

Floral wallpaper covered the walls. I tried to notice everything, anything to help me understand her.

No one else seemed to be home.

"We have to be quiet," she said, "my mom's sleeping."

So much for being alone with her.

"Sure. We often take Sunday naps too."

She smiled, a little nervously I thought, and sat down. "I'm having trouble finding a topic." She lifted a notebook. "I started this on the Soviet Union in Afghanistan, but I didn't get far."

"Why not choose something you already know about? Or something topical." I pulled out my draft on farm policies. "If you choose a familiar topic, you can bring in your own experiences or thoughts. You don't have to rely totally on research. That's what I did."

She sighed and raised her eyebrows. "Any suggestions?"

I shrugged. Then I remembered the Sunday school lesson. "How about some school issue, like alcoholism among the young, drinking in school, stuff like that?"

She pursed her lips and glanced off for a moment and I noted her straight nose and perfect chin—what a beautiful profile.

"You know," I continued eagerly, "you could interview other kids. Or cover alcoholism in America, drunk driving, stuff like that."

"I think I like the idea about drinking in schools," she said quickly.

"You could even limit your topic to Hillcrest."

We then came up with possible areas to explore. Once I got her started, her ideas really flowed. About 4 o'clock I heard Mrs. Johnson come down. I didn't see her, but Melanie called out that we were in the study. I was surprised at how quickly the time had passed.

"Fine," replied her mother from the kitchen. Shortly, I heard some hot water on the stove and later smelled coffee.

"Would you like anything?" her mom called.

"No," said Melanie, then, "sure." She left abruptly and returned with some pop for us.

About 5 o'clock I gathered my papers. I wanted to stay longer but figured they'd be having supper soon. The time had gone much too quickly.

"I don't know how to thank you," Melanie said at the door, her blue eyes looking up at me, seeming to search my face.

I wanted to reply: You could go out with me.

Instead: "Glad to help."

I left, feeling both happy and sad and puzzled. I think that I love her but I know that I've missed my chance.

Saturday: The school hosted a junior varsity boys and girls BB tournament today. Since Dad had to work today, I went along, thinking that maybe I could help him. He liked my company, but he needed no assistance.

After the tournament, Dad complained bitterly. "It's not that I mind the money, but I have nothing to do. It's boring. Open the doors. Wait around to see if anyone needs to get to a locker. It's not real work."

He complains more and more about his job. I don't think he'll last long as a custodian. I hope that he can find something he enjoys.

In the future, I want to work at something I enjoy. I've been thinking more and more about college. Guess I should attend one, maybe Rochester Community College, picking up some business classes, then get a trade at Vo-tech. I've decided that a person can only sheetrock so long before he either joins management or claims disability.

I would enjoy managing a business, I think. But, whatever it is, I want to do something where I can see results.

Sunday: Pastor Jim nabbed me again after church (I skipped Sunday school). He's planning several winter activities. A group of students is meeting before the PM service—would I like to be involved?

I said I'd like to go to some of their activities but that I was too busy to commit myself to anything yet. My schedule was up in the air with work and maybe the one-act. Set the plans, I told him, and I could probably attend something.

Sometimes he can be so pushy . . . . To be honest, I really can't say that. He's interested in getting me involved, so I call him pushy. If he ignored me I'd call him uncaring. I guess I like to complain. Maybe all people do. Complaining gives me a reason not to do something, not to be involved. Truthfully, I just don't want to get entangled in church. "To be a Christian means you're an outsider to the world," Pastor Jim once said.

I don't know if I want to be an outsider.

Monday: Aaron sought me out this morning before anyone else came to our table in the commons.

"I'm going to break up with Jen," he stated.

I felt as if he'd thrown cold water in my face. I recovered from my shock, nodded, and said nothing. I refused to get involved in his decision. I continued working on my math.

"I think I'll do it after Christmas."

My quick mouth—I couldn't stop it! "Why wait?" I blurted.

"Maybe you're right," he said, looking down the empty hall. "It would be harder after we'd exchanged gifts. Best to do it now. Clean break."

The others filtered in. When the bell rang, Aaron walked off with an air of self-assurance and purpose.

Tomorrow will tell.

After school Mr. Richter trained me in at Hillcrest Pizza. He was really patient, though he doesn't look it. He's short and squat and with his bushy eyebrows and slight German accent, he initially gives the impression that he's quite stern. He said his parents brought him to America when he was a kid.

"And then the 1960's came and did they think they'd made a mistake!" He shook his head and laughed at some memory.

It all seemed too long ago to me, but I smiled, nodded, and acted as if I understood.

He went through all the pizza measurements and showed me where they're written down. The sauce recipe is supposed to be top secret. For now he will make the sauce and crusts and handle the cash register, and I'll put on the pizza toppings and operate the oven.

I appreciated how clearly he explained things. It made me feel good about working there. He knew exactly what he wanted and didn't put on any pretence. I guess you have to be what you seem to be in order to be successful as a business in a small town. People see through phonies right away. Small towns have few secrets.

Tuesday: I worked extra hours today—not much time to write.

Miss G. asked if I'd act in the play. She was short an actor—would I do it?

"I'd rather run lights," I said. "And I've just started a new job."

"We'll work around it," she said. "If you want to, that is. We've edited the play, you know, so your part would be quite small, not many rehearsals. I think you could play the part of Curley perfectly."

I hesitated.

"Talk to the rest of the cast," she said. "See what they think. The list is posted outside my door."

I hurried past her room to beat the bell, and I glanced at her list. Melanie Johnson—Curley's Wife.

I knew then what I'd do, but I couldn't seem too willing. I'll tell her tomorrow that I can help her out.

Wednesday: I worked extra hours again. I stand almost the whole time and I feel it in my legs, but the ache's not too bad. Good thing I like the aroma of pizza.

In school I told Miss G. I'd be in the play, and I gave her my work schedule.

She gave me the cut script for *Of Mice and Men.* My part—Curley—doesn't have too many lines. He shouts and generally acts like a jerk. Miss G. says I have a strong voice for the part. (I hope it's not because she thinks I make a good jerk!) I'm only on stage for a few minutes—about the same as I was for Mr. Gibbs.

After vacation, she'll prepare a practice schedule. We're supposed to have lines memorized by then.

Bob S. is in the play (George) and Cliff Jorgenson plays Lennie. I don't know Cliff too well, but during football I know they called him "The Line." He should do well with the part.

Thursday: After school Miss G. had a brief organizational meeting.

Bob S. invited me to a Christmas party next Tuesday. I said I'd try to be there.

Then I dashed to work and made pizzas until 8 o'clock. I ate a pizza for supper—a nice fringe benefit.

Did some school work and here it is, 10 o'clock.

Now I know what they mean by "rat race."

Friday: Thought I'd never make it. I'm exhausted from work—Friday's a wild evening—but life's going so great that I have to write about it.

After Christmas my days to work will be Tues., Weds., and Fridays. Mr. Richter made it very clear that school comes first and I'm to let him know if I fall behind in my assignments. I doubt other employers are as understanding.

I saw Melanie at H. Pizza tonight. She ate with several of the cheerleaders before the game. Her uniform fit her well.

When she came up to the counter, she smiled at me. I suddenly felt confident.

"Say, Melanie," I began, trying to sound casual, "would you like to go with me to a party next Tuesday?"

She looked at me for a moment, surprised. I was sure that she'd say no, but she smiled bigger and said yes.

Life's going great. My first check. My first official date with the most beautiful girl in Hillcrest.

Sunday: What a turnaround this afternoon has been.

Saturday I was busy around the house helping Mom and Amy put Christmas decorations up. I was so energetic I jumped out of bed the next morning for Sunday school. I even participated in the class discussion on pre-marital sex. (Some of the girls stared at their feet during most of the lesson. I don't think Mary Arnold ever looked up.)

The Bible, I knew, is clearly against sex outside of marriage and Pastor Jim brought out most of the relevant verses. My parents have always stressed that God intended sex to be within marriage. To put it before a marriage confuses priorities, destroys true communication, creates guilt. I wondered—and said so in class—if it was always so absolute.

"Why do people have sex before marriage?" Pastor Jim asked.

No one answered, of course. Guess it was one of those rhetorical questions pastors and teachers like to toss out.

"Usually it is to satisfy personal physical drives without a commitment to the other person. Premarital sex is a selfish act if you don't wait for marriage. You're not thinking of the other person, but yourself. Besides that, on the spiritual level, premarital sex says to God that you don't trust Him, that you want to be in charge of your own life, have the things you want when you want it. Remember that God created sex, but said it needs to be in the confines of the marriage commitment."

I'm not sure I agree with him 100%, but I couldn't refute it.

Anyway, all my questions and energy have vanished.

Melanie called about 4 o'clock this afternoon. When she called, I was outside shoveling the driveway. According to Mom, Melanie didn't want to pull me from my work so she left a message.

She canceled our date Tuesday night.

I had Mom repeat the message twice.

"Melanie said that some things have come up and she just can't make it to the party."

I didn't know a heart could hurt so much.

I snacked on cheese curls all night.

I can't write any more. I'm still depressed.

Monday: A hard day at school. I finished my assignments but without enthusiasm or quality. At work I nearly burned two pizzas and I know I put too much sauce on several. Mr. Richter, showing his first hint of anger, pointed the second one out to me.

At work I saw Melanie. She smiled at me cheerfully as if nothing had happened.

I nodded to her, smiling back. She was right. Nothing had.

I called Sarah after work, asked if she'd like to go. It was short notice, I knew, but I wanted to go with someone, to save some kind of face, if only to myself.

"Are his parents going to be there?"

Oops.

"I didn't ask," I confessed. "Sorry."

"That's fine," she replied cheerfully. "Can I let you know tomorrow?"

"Sure," I said. Maybe some hope lies over the horizon.

Somehow, though, I doubt it. I can't see the horizon in town.

Tuesday: Writing tonight, with Christmas three days away, I should be happy.

Bad news right away. In the morning Sarah sat at our table and told me she couldn't go. Her parents had called Swansons. No, Bob's mother informed, they weren't going to be there but were sure things would be fine. She stated that Bob was very responsible and only a few kids had been invited.

"Without a parent there, I can't go," Sarah explained. "I'm sorry. I would like to go, but that's my parents for you."

"Oh," I shrugged, looking down. I know she would've gone elsewhere with me, maybe was hoping I'd ask, but I wanted to go to that party. To be invited by Bob Swanson meant something. "Maybe next time," I said.

"Okay," she said and worked on some homework. I felt like a real heel, but I was going to go, even by myself.

School went quickly. The day before vacation is always wild.

After work I drove out to Bob's, arriving about 8:15. As I walked up the steps, I heard loud music rhythmically vibrating through the walls. I had to knock loudly—practically pound on the door—before Bob ushered me in. He grinned broadly. I headed to the basement.

The only light came from the VCR but no one could hear it because the stereo was blasting. Kids were sprawled all over the floor, on the sofa, on the chairs. Someone handed me a cold can of pop, I took a sip—funny-tasting—looked again. Beer.

A collection of empty cans filled a corner wastebasket. I stared at the cold beer in my hand, at the empty cans.

Bob came down the steps, noticed me, and explained. "We've been collecting beer for a week. Tonight we'll pitch the empties on the road. Just don't spill, and my parents won't suspect a thing." He looked around at the scattered kids. "Now this is a true party."

I see now why the Websters called Bob's mother. They knew what the Swansons didn't—or wouldn't—acknowledge. In the dim, flickering, colored light from the television, I spied Aaron and Jennifer over on the sofa, she perched on his lap. Both were drinking. I never suspected that Aaron (or Jennifer) drank.

(Looking back—How was I so blind? I arrived at the same answer: all the work Dad gave us on the farm kept us that way.)

Aaron spotted me, overcame his surprise, waved me over.

Jennifer leaned forward, allowed his hand to slip down her back and then up her sweater. She giggled.

She saw me, leaned back. "Hey, Chad!" she called, "welcome to the party. Merry Christmas."

"Merry Christmas," I echoed, walking carefully so as not to step on anyone.

"Sit down," said Jennifer. Her bleary eyes tried to focus on me. The two, giggling, awkwardly made room. I sat on the sofa, wedged between them and some big, red-headed guy from Cherry Grove who was talking to Lisa Overlund and some other girls sitting on the floor.

"No date?" Aaron asked.

What could I say? "No."

"I talked to Melanie the other day," said Jennifer. "She was pretty down. She and a guy over in Cherry Grove—Jay—officially broke up."

"I thought she was going out with some other guy."

"Oh, that was nothing. Anyway, after she broke up with Jay, I told her to keep her date with you, that you were a really nice guy."

Embarrassed, I smiled awkwardly. "Thanks. But I guess she didn't."

She held in a burp, giggled. "I guess."

I turned to the movie, more to avoid her and the conversation than to see what was going on.

The movie showed two little kids peering through a bathroom curtain at a naked woman. I'm sure if the lights had been on, everyone would've seen my face blush brighter than Rudolph's nose. Even my neck felt hot. On the floor, several people laughed.

I never did catch the plot, if there was one. Lots of naked women running around, a few car chases, several sex scenes under blankets, several later without the blankets.

Not sure what else to do, I took a few hesitant sips of beer. The only time I'd had alcohol was sampling my dad's annual can on the Fourth of July and a glass of champagne on New Year's. That was all the alcohol I'd ever had.

This party made me feel like a real innocent.

Melanie had made me feel like a real fool.

People were guzzling the beer. Several had brought their own bottles of hard alcohol. Kids were constantly staggering into the room, lounging in front of the TV, squeezing closer to the stereo, slumping in the sofa, and shuffling out to other rooms in the basement.

I stayed where I was. Shortly, Aaron and Jennifer went somewhere, upstairs I guess, and I shifted to the corner spot.

I wanted to leave but didn't want to seem rude or stuck-up. I'm sure that's how some characterized Sarah.

A little later, a Hillcrest sophomore boy and a girl I didn't recognize sat on the sofa right next to me and began necking and petting.

I looked away. I couldn't believe they'd do that right in front of others. No one else seemed to care.

I saw Bob, the smiling host, move from place to place throughout the night, checking on people, I guess.

Still later, about the time the video ended, I heard the large, red-headed guy from Cherry Grove talking about coke.

After a few more of his comments, I realized that it wasn't the pop.

It was time to go.

Getting to my feet, I gingerly walked over the crowd on the floor to the stairs.

I hadn't seen Aaron and Jennifer since they'd left. Gone home, I figured.

Lisa Overlund seemed to come out of nowhere and sidled up to me. She's short and slightly plump, also a senior. I've known her since kindergarten. In grade school art we often used to color together. I hadn't talked to her for years.

She grabbed my arm. She was drunk. She leaned close to me, pushed her breasts against my hand.

"Hi, Chad. I was wondering when you'd move from that corner." Her strong breath made me blink.

I hesitated. "Hi, Lisa." My hands were sweaty.

"Time for another drink? In the other room?"

"Well, I better get going," I said nervously.

"So soon? Only 11? Bob's folks won't be home 'till 1:00 in the morning. We have 'till midnight to clean up."

"I really should go," I said again.

"I thought you were great in the play," she muttered. Then she giggled at something. "Wanna go over some lines in the next room where we can be by ourselves?"

I didn't say anything. I didn't know what to say or do.

She squinted her eyes and suddenly looked offended. "You're not gay or anything, are you?"

I know I blushed scarlet. I felt embarrassed and angry and pressured.

"My parents are expecting me." Then I lied: "Lots of work around the house tomorrow, you know."

"Oh." She ran her hand around my back, up under my sweater. "If you gotta go. But the other room is available now, for a short time." She leaned against me. "I've got one, if you didn't come prepared."

My mouth was dry. I don't know what I said but I got out fast, passing Bob on the steps.

"Thanks for inviting me," I said.

"Oh, Chad," he said. "I forgot to tell you. I hate to even mention it, but most of the kids chip in two bucks for the drinks."

"Sure. I understand." I lied again, reaching for my wallet.

"No. This is your first official Bob Swanson party." He grinned, patting my shoulder like a used car salesman. "Next time."

I don't recall driving home. I don't even remember coming in the door, but I do recall the warm, encompassing sense of relief, of shelter.

I'm really confused.

New Year's Eve: Vacation's almost over, vacation from school, assignments, thinking and writing.

I haven't done that lately.

Writing, that is.

I couldn't.

Many things need to be sorted out in my mind. Kids I have gone to school with for years . . . I've looked behind their school masks and found other faces.

In my sheltered home and life I assumed others were like me.

They're not.

Perhaps in their minds no deception exists. They act a certain way with adults, another when in their cliques.

Question: Is it wrong to drink? Aaron, who I've always admired, drank heavily.

The law says 21. So what? I ask myself. Adults ignore the speed limits all the time. Politicians ignore their own laws.

"Be not drunk with wine but filled with the Holy Spirit." A nice thought, but is it realistic? Is it even possible?

Answer: I don't know.

Question: Are drugs wrong? I thought cocaine was only in the inner cities.

Drugs are dangerous, foolish, suicidal. Yet no one seemed to be in danger, no drug deaths have occurred in Hillcrest.

Answer: I'm not sure.

Question: Sex?

Some kids have done it. Illegitimate births occur all the time. They always have. I know what my parents have taught me. But society says love (whatever that is) makes sex okay. And movies show that you don't even need the love first, that sex is okay anytime. Sometimes people only date once or twice before going to bed.

What about the new AIDS, or other diseases? I've never heard anyone seriously worry about it. Those things always happen to others.

Pastor Jim calls premarital sex selfish.

Is that what society is? (Another question.)

Answer to the first question: I'm confused. I think back to Lisa's invitation to the other room. In the safety of my bedroom, my curiosity outweighs my fear. I get excited. I could have gone with her. Maybe quite easily.

Question: Should I?

Answer: No. It would've been selfish to satisfy a desire. I guess I do accept what Pastor Jim says. It makes sense.

Was she attracted to me? Or did a friend put her up to it? I certainly don't love her, I don't even know her well.

What is love anyway? I think I know what lust is . . . or do I?

More questions. No answers.

Better write about something else . . . .

Our family Christmas was nice, though I felt out of it. Mom and Dad noticed my moodiness. Amy, of course, didn't.

We had our traditional candlelit Christmas Eve dinner and exchanged gifts.

Mom and Dad gave me a nice electric typewriter. It's a used one from school and very solid. It'll be great for college (or will everyone have word processors?) Amy gave me some after-shave that I'm sure Mom picked out.

Question: I know my family observes the birth of Christ, but why do others celebrate? What does it mean to them? A time to get drunk? To party?

The next day, Christmas, we went to the cousins. Grandpa was there too. We had a good time and a big meal, but my spirit was still confused. My heart still hurt from Melanie.

A new year begins tomorrow.

I should be happy. 1985. The year I graduate.

Wednesday: Half week of school. The first day back in school went well. Everyone else seemed to want to talk at once and was—believe it or not—glad to be back. Not that anyone missed assignments, but everyone wanted to reestablish the social ties that so often center on school.

I compensated for my confusion by working harder. I turned out two small articles today, handed in my term paper, and outworked everyone in building trades. I then dashed to a short play practice (didn't get a chance to talk to Melanie), then off to work.

After I got home, Pastor Jim called on the phone. He's starting a Wednesday evening Bible study. I told him I couldn't make it because of all the things I'm involved in. He sounded discouraged. It must be hard to get kids together when we're all busy.

Sitting here and looking back and thinking hard, I've just decided two things: First, I'm going to ask Melanie out again. Secondly, I'm not going to be frightened off by other students. I want to learn how I should live and what I should be committed to. I have my chance. I'm not going to run away.

Thursday: Since I didn't have to work tonight, I was able to stay for all of play practice. The one-act is really interesting. Loneliness is the theme. As Miss G. explains the play, it's about losers. All the characters are looking for something and not finding it. Then the question remains for the audience to answer: Does George do the right thing by killing Lennie?

Maybe I could develop it into an interesting editorial-combined-with-publicity article?

Anyway, I talked to Melanie. I followed her to her locker, told her she did a good job.

"Thanks, Chad. It's really hard, y'know, acting that way."

She does a good job, though, giving the "come on" to the guys. She's a perfect choice. But I couldn't tell her that in a diplomatic way.

She grabbed her books out of her locker.

"Say, Melanie, would you like to go to a movie Saturday?"

She paused a moment. "I don't know." She turned to face me, hugging her books to herself, creating a wall between us. "I'm so busy with everything."

I persisted. "If not Saturday, another night next week?"

She shifted her weight, glanced down the empty hall. I was determined to get an answer from her.

She looked back at me. "How about just getting a snack after the game Friday?" she offered. I felt that I was being tossed a handful of crumbs, but I took it.

"Better than nothing," I grinned nonchalantly. "But I have to work longer this Friday, until 10:00." I wasn't going to wear my heart completely on my sleeve. "Could you come down after the game and I'll buy you a coke, maybe some pizza?"

"Okay," she said.

That was it.

I'm not going to build up my hopes this time.

Friday: I half expected her not to show up, but she did about three minutes after ten. She seemed a little edgy, maybe tired. I wiped off the back counter.

Even though she may not be interested in me, I was determined to have an understanding between us, an honest and open relationship, romantic or otherwise.

(I guess that's why I keep this journal—it keeps me honest with myself.)

She looked my way, slipped out of her coat, and sat down. I hung up my apron, wrote down my time, joined her.

I ordered a small pizza and Pepsi. Pizza was free, pop wasn't.

"Don't your legs get cold in that cheerleading outfit?" I sat across from her.

"Sometimes," she said. "We keep moving and try not to think about it."

(I wonder—is that her life philosophy—move quickly and don't think?)

We both looked around at who was in the place. Several groups of younger kids were coming in. A lot of upper classmen had already left for Rochester.

She told me about the game but I wasn't listening. I tried to memorize her appearance: Oval face. Clear complexion. Soft hair. Bright blue eyes. Delicate lips. This might be the last time I'd have to be "alone" with her.

"Melanie," I finally said, fingering my cold glass of pop. "I'm sorry to pester you, but I just thought it would be fun to go out—"

She broke in. "And I'm sorry I canceled our date before Christmas. It's just that—"

Mr. Richter brought our pizza over. He winked at me, slipped me the tab, face down.

She burned her mouth on the first bite but soon ate quickly, hungrily. After we'd downed a few pieces of the pizza, she explained: "Chad, I like you. I appreciate your help. But I was going with a guy and we broke up right before you asked me out. I thought, okay, I'll go out with Chad. But the more I thought about it, the more I was afraid that, well, I didn't want a rebound."

"A what?"

"I'm afraid that I'd rebound into another relationship."

I was shocked, surprised, flabbergasted. "I just wanted to go out," I stammered. "Have a fun time doing something."

"I know," she said. "But it might get to be more than that."

She stared at the remaining pieces of pizza. I didn't know if I was being told the truth. She was afraid to go out with me because she might fall in love with me? Did I hear that right?

"I like you," I said, not sure anymore what I really felt. "And I thought I'd like to get to know you better. Hey, canceling our date was no big deal," I lied. I shrugged. I sipped my Pepsi. Right or wrong, good idea or bad, that's what I said.

"We're friends," she said. "Let's keep it that way."

Was this a fancy brush-off? A "good friends" speech?

"Sure."

Mr. Richter started to close up. We stood. I helped her with her coat. "But if you'd like to go out some time, just let me know."

Good idea or bad, that's what I said. The ball was in her court.

She let it stay there.

I picked up the tab. Mr. Richter had written "No Charge" with a smiling face. I wished my heart matched his drawing. We left. I drove her home.

That was it.

Good night.

Saturday: Pastor Jim organized an impromptu (Mrs. W. would be proud of my vocab!) game of broomball. Everyone had a good time. Including me. It seemed like a long time since I'd enjoyed myself.

Afterwards we went over to his parsonage for hot chocolate. Steve was very talkative—especially with the girls. He's starting to come out of his shell. The fall play was good for him in that way. (How do others see me—in a shell or out?)

I felt sorry for Walter. He talks a lot and everyone is friendly, but he just doesn't fit in. Maybe he tries too hard?

Pastor Jim got a "sure" out of me when he asked if I'd be in Sunday school tomorrow.

He brings you into his house for chocolate, then commits you to getting up early. What a gimmick.

Sunday: After church we went to see Grandpa. He wasn't feeling well, his face was haggard and pale, and his breathing was raspy.

The county nursing home, though brightly painted, still smells of catheters. It's depressing. Gathered in one place are old people with no way out but one. I have life ahead of me, but theirs is mostly behind them.

In his room, Grandpa slouched in his favorite vinyl easy chair. He's fairly short and thin and has a long, prominent nose. He's mostly bald, except for wispy tufts along the sides and back. We asked about his health and he went on awhile about that. He also rambled on about some of the other residents. His hearing is mostly gone; whenever we wanted to talk to him, we had to shout. In his wheezing voice, he asked how school was going for Amy and me. I told him about the new play. I don't think he remembers the last one.

I've always liked him. Even with his health problems now, that hasn't changed. Nor has his attitude. He still is interested in us, says he prays for us every day. When he dies, I know God will welcome him into heaven.

What'll happen when I die?

Better go to sleep before I get morbid.

Monday: Counselor called me into his office today. Mr. Warner is about fifty years old and heavy-set. To be honest: fat. He has a wide face, double chin, and gray hair combed over his bald top. He wears half-glasses for reading. He usually acts so busy, too busy to talk about real problems with the students, but he does manage to guide kids to further education—those who want it.

I sat down. He acted as business-like as always.

"Chad, I called you in because I ran across your test scores again and looked up your grades. You're enrolled in reading class next semester."

"I need an English credit."

"How's journalism going? I've seen your articles. Nice editorials you and Melanie put together."

"We make a good team."

"That's nice." He shuffled some papers on his desk, pulled out one and handed it to me. It was his way of saying: Let's get down to business.

"Chad, look at your scores. You already read quite well. This course isn't for you."

"I know I read alright, but I need an English credit."

"True." He handed me a registration booklet with a course circled. I looked at it.

"College prep? That's hard."

He half-smiled: "A challenge. I think you should take it."

"Why?"

"It'll prepare you for college. Students do a lot of vocabulary work. A lot of writing too, which you're seeming to manage. The class also surveys English literature."

"But I don't know if I'm going to college."

"The class would still be good for you." He leaned back in his swivel chair. "Students in that class don't complain about tough material—the work load maybe—but not the content. But I have had other students complain in other classes that they're bored."

I hedged.

He persisted. "I've read your articles and I know what Melanie writes by herself. You ask the questions. You have an inquiring mind, not the typical high school 'Why do we have to do this stuff?' attitude, but you pose real questions that probe for answers, deep answers. I don't see much of that in high school." He glanced out the window for a split second. "I don't see much of that in life, either. It's a rare gift." His speech delivered, he leaned forward and laid his hands on his papers. His fingertips touched.

I wasn't sure.

"You might make—probably would make—more money in a trade, but you won't be satisfied. Your creativity demands something more. A college degree might be essential some day."

"For what?"

He shrugged evasively. "I don't know. You've had a change of plans. Life's diverting you elsewhere. I think for your own good you need to keep your options open, get the best education you can." He slid a change of course form across his desk to me.

"You won't regret it," he stated.

"Is that a promise?" I replied, smiling.

"Well," he hedged, chuckling a bit. "This year you might, but a year from now you won't."

"Guaranteed?"

"Guaranteed."

I signed up. I'm a sucker for flattery.

Tuesday: Blizzard hit southern Minnesota like a white hurricane. Frigid wind rattled the windows while snow filled in the streets. Traffic was non-existent.

Wednesday: No school again today. The blizzard finally died around noon and the long shoveling began. Boy, did my back ache!

I went to work this evening. Only a few people out. Snow drifted down Main Street like sand dunes. The orders we had were mostly "to go." Everyone hibernates in weather like this.

The wind is picking up again. All the new dry snow will really blow in the country.

Maybe another day off?

Thursday: Only a late start this morning, but I enjoyed sleeping in.

Play practice went well. The cast is getting into the parts. Melanie is fascinating. She moves with such grace and intensity. Her blues eyes flash, and I can't keep my eyes off her. Is it lust or love? I don't know enough about either, I guess.

End of quarter tomorrow. Lots of tests. Better study.

Friday: School was wild and my mind feels as dry as an old bone. Tests and more tests. Even in building trades.

Work was crazy—huge crowds piled in after the game.

I'll sleep well tonight. That's all.

Saturday: After our broomball game, Steve, Walter, and Aaron came over for hot chocolate and Mom's homemade cinnamon rolls. Aaron hung around after the other guys left. We went up to my room and listened to some records.

I've been spending more time with Steve and Walter and have hardly talked to Aaron since Christmas. He seemed discouraged, almost depressed. I figured it had to do with Jennifer. I asked him how things were going.

He looked down, sat on my bed, sighed. "On again, off again. Each time I talk about seeing other girls, she gets really funny, then she gets affectionate."

I sure had no advice for him!

"That night at Bob Swanson's party she was like that." This was the first time he mentioned the party. He never actually said he saw me at Bob's. I've decided that no one talks about parties of that kind, except to say something like "great party." Kids often act as if they had never done anything there with anyone else. When I saw Lisa afterwards, she was friendly—her usual self—but never said anything about the party. Some unwritten law keeps kids from talking about those experiences—at least in public.

I asked how things were right now.

He shrugged.

"Do you love her?"

He shrugged again, then looked up as if he hadn't thought of it before. "She's okay."

What was that supposed to mean? Could Aaron—who dated many girls before Jennifer and has been going out with her so long—not know what love is? If he didn't know, how could I figure it out?

We listened to more music and talked some more, but that was the closest we came to solving Aaron's problem.

*   *   *

SECOND SEMESTER, FIRST QUARTER

Monday: I hadn't asked who taught college prep English. Was I surprised (and glad) that it was Miss Gunderson! She'll make any class, no matter how boring, endurable.

The play keeps improving. I won't be able to make practices the rest of the week, so Miss G. worked extensively on my scenes. Each time we go through it, I feel more comfortable. Of course all I do (as Curley) is act angry. That's not too tough.

It's getting late. Lots of homework tonight. Working at Hillcrest Pizza has taught me that I have to study ahead.

Tuesday: Melanie and I are working on an editorial (which also includes some publicity) based on the one-act. We're examining the issue surrounding George's murder of Lennie.

The more I think of it, I'm convinced that life is not (no pun intended) a "dead end." Melanie, however, isn't sure. I guess that's why we work well together, why I like her—opposites attract.

For that matter, though, the attraction is only one-way. She's friendly, happy, and relaxed around me, more so even than around other students, but, for whatever reasons, she wants to be just "friends." I know I'm not that good looking, but I'm not that ugly. I know that my nose is too big and my hair is unruly, but otherwise I'm pretty normal. Maybe that's the trouble—a great-looking girl like her knows she can attract the best. Why bother with the average? Yet what's so great about Jay? His basketball skills are only going to take him so far, then he'll be left wondering what to do with his future, not unlike what I faced when we lost the farm.

Better get back to the article before I drown in self-pity. Steinbeck's ending is emotionally moving but logically twisted. I think George was wrong. He should've escaped with Lennie, defended him, seen he was given some kind of mental help. (Of course, Steinbeck stacks the cards against him.)

Oh well, it's just fiction.

Wednesday: Report cards were handed out today. Three A's (building trades, journalism, and government), an A—in chemistry, and the rest were B's. Best report card in my life!

Also, I talked with Aaron this morning in school, before the others showed up. He told me, in a hushed voice, that he had broken up with Jennifer.

"How did she take it?"

He looked down, frowning. "Not so good. I expected as much. She cried, then got angry, then cried some more, then told me it didn't matter."

"Well, it was best you did it now since you had made up your mind."

He glanced around at the empty halls and the banners hanging on the walls, almost looking like a lost kid at the county fair. He rubbed his pointed chin.

"Say," I suggested, "what about going to the game in Paradise tomorrow?"

He brightened up. "Why not?"

A short time later, when Steve, Walter, and Sarah showed up, I asked if we should all go. Everyone was interested, including Sarah.

Dad said I could take the car so it's all set for tomorrow. I suppose I should pick up Sarah first so the three other guys can all sit in the back seat. It'll be uncomfortable for Steve in the back with his long legs but I don't know how well she'd like to be crammed in the back seat with three guys.

Sarah's easy to be with. She doesn't seem to mind being the only girl. Of course, if I was (or is it "were"?) the only guy with four girls, I wouldn't mind either.

Thursday: It's late. Both boys and girls teams won the double-header. We all had fun together.

When I picked up Sarah, I walked to her door to meet her. Her dad met me at the door and invited me in. Since it was a group going to the game, I didn't feel nervous talking to him. It wasn't like I was taking her on a date. (Now that I think about it, he seemed to go out of his way to be friendly. I wonder if Sarah told him that he intimidated me.)

Mrs. Webster was sitting in the living room, reading. That helped me feel comfortable since I'm on pretty good terms with her.

At the game we saw Jennifer sitting among a group of girls. She glared at Aaron and then at Sarah for a long time. It was the kind of stare that teachers give to rowdy kids. I'm not sure what it all meant, but I guessed that she was jealous of Sarah. In fact, several girls gave her unnaturally long stares.

I mentioned it to her as we went back to our seats between quarters.

She laughed. "I'll catch it tomorrow at school. Four guys on a date—stuff like that."

"Oh." I offered her some popcorn.

I felt kind of funny, almost jealous. I leaned close to her, whispering, "Would you like to cut the odds down on Snow Week?"

She looked at me with those dark eyes, smiling innocently. "What do you mean?"

"Would you like to go with me to the Snow Dance in two weeks?"

Playfully, she pretended shock, grabbing my arm as if she were going to faint. "So far in advance? Tonight was planned just yesterday!"

"Well," I smiled, "I have to get my order in early to avoid this crowd."

She smiled. "Sure."

We hardly spoke for the rest of the evening. She was pleasant to everyone, even Walter. That's just the way she is. A good friend.

Friday: Just got home from work and I'm beat! Big one-act week coming up: perform on Thursday for town, Friday for school assembly, Saturday for judges.

I dreamt about the farm last night. I was sitting by the rock pile, counting cattle on the hillside below. The numbers kept changing, and I had to keep recounting. The vibrant sunset splashed amber and rose across the sky, but I couldn't look at it because I had to get the cattle counted.

It was a frustrating dream. Throughout the day, I thought about it.

I miss the farm.

Saturday: A lot of tension between Mom and Dad. The day started with good news—blizzard coming Sunday or Monday (we're all still pulling for Monday!) and Mom fixed us a big eggs-and-bacon breakfast: it reminded me of how we used to eat on the farm.

Everything was okay until mid-morning. Since I am the only one tall enough, I was resetting the kitchen clock that is constantly losing time when Mom asked Dad if he could fix the leak under the sink.

She smiled sincerely. "I'm just reminding you."

Evidently, Dad took it otherwise. "Of course I'll fix it," he snapped.

"I know you will." Her smile trembled a bit. "I was just afraid you'd forget."

Maybe he had forgotten and felt guilty. Maybe he hadn't and felt hassled. "Fix this, fix that," he mocked.

She probably should've let him wander off, muttering to himself, but she didn't. "Then don't fix it," she stated.

He stormed over to the sink. I stepped aside. He knelt,

violently swinging open the doors. "Why not? I follow orders at school everyday. Might as well at home, too."

Mom turned away in tears. She threw the dishcloth onto the counter and ran upstairs. The one thing Mom has always said is that she never wants to be a nag.

With his quick sarcasm, Dad had stabbed her in the heart.

He looked up at me from his kneeling position and shook his head. "Women are so touchy," he observed.

I glared at him for a moment, puzzled, shocked. I wanted to say something witty, something to show him his hypocrisy, something that would cut him as deeply as he had cut Mom, but no words came.

For the rest of the day, Mom's eyes were red.

Dad was surly.

Sunday: Slept in.

Played broomball in the afternoon. As we waited for the other team to bring the ball down the field, Steve walked over to me. His boots crunched on the snow.

"Missed you in church today," Steve said, his breath white in the cold air.

"Oh, I just overslept," I said, not adding that I had meant to. Our whole family had overslept.

When the going gets tough, sometimes you just stay away.

Even as I write this, the wind is picking up. Our storm windows are rattling. Outside, drifts of new snow are forming over the sidewalk and across the street.

The signs are strong for a wind-whipping Minnesota white-out blizzard!

Monday: No school today!

The blizzard lifted late morning. Everyone began the long process of digging out. I was surprised that some drifts in our backyard were up to my chest. Of course that's nothing compared to what we had in the country where drifts used to be over my head.

Dad tells the story of how he once was coming home in a blizzard and the car died right as he was turning into our lane. He had to leave it and walk home. If the yard light hadn't been on, he wouldn't have known the right direction. The next day the only reason the plow didn't hit the car was because at the last minute the driver saw the car's antenna sticking out of a drift and swerved away.

After today's storm died down, Dad walked to school to plow the parking lots and shovel out the entrances. While I was shoveling our back sidewalk (it was that hard-packed snow you get in strong winds), he drove up in the school plow and cleaned out our driveway.

My back ached by that time, so he was a welcome sight. That job of his does have some nice benefits.

Tuesday: Everyone was hoping the winds would pick up again but no such luck. It got warmer today, melting a bit of the snow.

School's really dragging now. I can see why the student council sponsors their Snow Week activities to break up the monotony.

The one-act play continues to progress well, even though we have to squeeze rehearsals around basketball practices and games. Miss G. gave us her regular (so Bob S. tells me) pep talk. "Do the best you can, but don't worry about the judges or about the results. Their job is to judge the best they can, and ours is to put on the best show we can."

"Do you think we'll get first?" I asked.

She crossed her arms and sat on the edge of her desk. "I've seen good plays get second or third while poor plays have won. Then again some years I agree with the judges. You just never know. Unfortunately, the results are only as valid as the judges' competence."

Melanie leaned towards me, poking me good-naturedly. "Just do the best we can," she smiled. My pulse picked up.

She still affects me the same way. No matter what happens, it will never be "just friends" with me.

Work went well today. I put in a little overtime.

Wednesday: A busy day. I was able to quit work early because of the dress rehearsal at 6 p.m. in the music room. The next time we do the play it'll be in front of the town on Thursday evening.

Mr. Richter has been extremely accommodating about letting me off early. "I support the arts," he always says. Today he complimented me: "Nice article in the school paper today. It gives us adults something to think about, this . . . er . . ."

"Euthanasia."

"Yah."

It makes me feel good, knowing adults think well of my writing.

Saturday: What an ending to the week.

Thursday's performance went well—except that we sprayed the hay with acrylic sealant meant to hold it in place and it didn't work too well and we ended up dropping hay all over the school.

Needless to say, the custodians—Dad included—weren't too sympathetic. Anyway, by Friday we had it solved by placing the hay on a huge sheet of fabric before moving it.

After Thursday's and Friday's performances, Miss G. answered questions from the audience. At both performances she was asked how she thought we'd do. It must be frustrating for directors of these contest plays. It's not supposed to be a competition, yet it is. People understand trophies.

Melanie and Bob were great and Cliff was, well, big. Afterwards many congratulated us. Even Bob said I was good. "You really show Curley up as the creep he is."

"I'll take that as a compliment," I laughed.

Saturday, Miss G. had us over for breakfast. Mr. Monroe helped her serve the meal (I wonder if the rumors are true that they're getting serious?) Then he drove the bus for us.

Mr. Monroe is a good teacher. He's average height, a little heavy set in the waist, and his hair is thinning. I would think Miss G. could do better. (Isn't it funny how we rate people by looks? I do it to others, but when I'm rated by looks, it's unfair.)

The play went smoothly on Saturday. Everyone was at his (or her) peak. Quite a few Hillcrest people came over to watch. Cliff's mom cried. It must be hard to see your son "killed" on stage.

We got second, though. We still advance to the regional contest next Saturday, but the second place trophy isn't like the first.

Miss G. was ecstatic. "I don't care," she said, "first or second. You'll get the experience of performing at Winona State University. That's what's valuable. You'll take that with you the rest of your life."

I don't know. I'd still rather be first.

On the ride home we read the judges' comments. Overall, they were pretty useless, I thought. One judge didn't like our transitional music (Miss G. intentionally picked it to be ironic.) He obviously didn't stop to think about it, didn't assume we knew what we were doing. Another judge (who ranked us third) said all these great things about us but didn't tell us what we should change.

Oh well, Miss G. said the one-act should be a learning experience. The play was. I'm not sure about the judging.

Sunday: The whole family went to Sunday school and church. Quite a few people at church seemed to know about the play already. Maybe Miss G. is right. Second was as good as first. In his announcements Pastor Jim congratulated the cast (and me) for our performance.

As we sat there in the pews, it occurred to me why dad had come to church again—his second time in a year. His attendance could only be because of the play. I was stunned. Dad wanted to be in church to "show me off."

He never did say anything to me. This was one time that his actions spoke louder than his voice.

Pastor Jim pulled me aside as we were filing out and asked if I'd help plan a winter retreat for the end of February, when regular season basketball games would be ending and just before the tournaments. There was a meeting next Sunday to plan.

I said I'd try to make it.

I think I was sincere.

Monday: Surprise. I was elected a Snow Week candidate. Me! Of course, two things helped. A winning one-act. (The trophy looked impressive in the office!) Secondly, no homecoming candidates were eligible. That meant that Bob, Steve and the others couldn't be nominated.

It's too bad Melanie was also eliminated. It would have been great to be "king and queen." (Why do I keep torturing myself with these fantasies?)

Mom and Dad were interested in how Snow Week worked. "Each class has two candidates," I explained, "one boy and one girl. The school has contests throughout the week between grades 10, 11, and 12. The winning team gets to have their [oops: "its"] candidate reign—the best boy's team gets the king, the winning girl's team the queen. You could have a senior king and a sophomore queen."

"Or the other way around," Amy teased. That was the first time she had said anything about it.

"Sure," I said. "The junior high classes also have their prince and princess royalty."

"I'm on the seventh grade volleyball and three-legged race teams," Amy announced.

"That's great," Mom said, patting her shoulder. "Two such popular children. What have I done to deserve this?"

"Just remember," Dad added, his need to make an announcement showing itself, "popularity isn't important. Honesty is."

Tuesday: Wouldn't you know? I woke up with a big red zit on my nose. And I mean big and red.

I dug the acne medicine out of the bathroom cabinet and have been covering the scarlet behemoth all day. My entire nose throbs. I tried to hide it with my hand most of the day.

At work the intense heat of the stove caused me to sweat off all the cover-up medicine. Tonight I'll really plaster it and hope it's gone tomorrow.

What a time for a beaner like this—snow week "crowning" on Friday, dance that night, play on Saturday.

Why me?

Wednesday: Now the zit's crusted with dry skin. It's so flaky that no covering will help. At least I didn't have to be in any activities today. During classes I could hide my nose. I found that chewing my pencil is a good reason to have my hand up.

It's been harder to hide it during play practice. Fortunately, I could only stay about twenty minutes before dashing off to work. I don't think Melanie had time to study my face.

Rudolph the red-nosed actor.

Thursday: Zit's finally clearing up. I'll probably have a purple scar the rest of my life. Seniors aren't supposed to have this problem, only sophomores!

Practice went well today. Next time we go through the play, we'll be at Winona State U.

Our boys' snow week team is ahead, the girls' is too close to call, but the queen will either be Sarah (juniors) or Lisa Overlund (seniors).

I'm glad the Snow Week activities disrupt all the classes. The teachers have lightened up on the homework. With all the things going on, I'm not sure how good my assignments would have been.

Both BB teams lost tonight. With sports on the slide, wouldn't it be great if the one-act pulled off a region trophy?

Friday: Very late.

"What've I done to deserve two popular kids?" Mom had said. Now she regrets that distinction. She wants to crawl into a hole and die.

As always, I'd best get the record straight from the start:

At the end of the day today, the school held an obstacle race. Among the high school boys, I came in second but we had enough points that the senior boys won anyway.

I was Snow Week King.

Among the girls the point totals were close between Lisa and Sarah but the obstacle course decided it. Sarah slipped on a tire. Lisa won and became queen.

Oh well.

The evening went fine at first. When I picked up Sarah, she was wearing a high-colored, long-sleeve blue dress as the "attendant" to Lisa. She looked stunning. Her long dark hair was like black velvet. I wore a pinstriped suit and tie. Both of us brought jeans along to change into after the Grand March. The chaperones always let royalty make a quick dash out to their cars to get a change of clothing.

At the dance they had a special program, put the spotlight on us, and made us read some silly pronouncements. (Be honest: Silly they were, but I was glad that I was the one reading them.) It was an all-school dance, grades 7 to 12, the only all-school dance other than homecoming that we have. Being snow king was quite an honor.

"You make a great king," Sarah whispered into my ear after the opening ceremony.

Lisa and I had to start the first dance. She wore a long white dress with a low-cut back. During the dance, they dimmed the lights and she pressed close to me and slipped her arms around my neck. Though her breath reeked of alcohol, she certainly acted normally.

Lisa pulled my neck down a bit, whispered: "I've got a little something in my car. Let's toast each other."

"Oh." I didn't want to go near her car but felt I should be polite, friendly. (Be honest: I was afraid to offend her. She has a big mouth for gossip and backbiting.)

The dance ended. The sound system DJ's put on a fast tape. I sat down on one of the folding chairs that were lined up along the edge of the gym. When younger I danced to those fast songs (we had real bands then), probably making a pretty good fool of myself. Around my sophomore year, I noticed how the younger kids all looked like uncoordinated grasshoppers. Few people can dance well, I determined, and I wasn't one of them.

Sarah approached, sat next to me. "Going to change?"

"A little later," I said. She wanted to change then, so I gave her the keys to the car. She was back in a minute, went to the girls' bathroom, and came out in sweater and jeans and tennis shoes.

I felt depressed.

"Anything wrong?" she asked, sitting beside me.

"No," I lied. I had crashed from the heights of royalty and felt like a peasant again. I realized that as soon as I changed, no one would remember I had been king. Secondly, the peasant was caught in a dilemma. Lisa was eyeing me from across the dark gym, waiting for me to go outside to get my other clothes. I knew then how a mouse felt when being eyed by a cat.

I had signed the high school league form about alcohol and drugs.

But so had Bob Swanson. That didn't stop him, didn't even slow him down.

Lisa had signed one to be in athletics. Breaking her word didn't faze her. Why was I so worried? It seems that whenever I do something wrong, I always get caught.

"Sarah," I said, desperate to change the direction of my thoughts. "What do you think you'll do after high school?"

The music was so loud that we had to shout into each other's ears.

"I was thinking of being a nurse," she shrugged. "Maybe."

"A big demand for them."

"But lousy pay for the responsibility. What about you? Reached any decisions yet?"

"No."

I glanced at her face. The colored lights from the sound system flashed in her brown eyes. She was really a very beautiful girl.

"If you still had the chance to farm, would you?"

For the first time it hit me, almost like jumping into a cold lake. I realized with complete clarity that I missed the farm, yet I wasn't sure if I still wanted to farm. I was changing so quickly. "I'm not sure," I finally said.

Our voices were getting hoarse from shouting, so we listened to the music for a while. The sound system DJ's started a slower number.

"Come on," she said, suddenly grabbing my hand.

What a different dancer she was from Lisa. Sarah moved gracefully, rhythmically. I think half the time she led, but I'm such a lousy dancer, I wouldn't even know for sure.

After the song, I headed for the door and Mr. Monroe. Lisa spied me and followed.

"Give you one minute," Mr. Monroe stated.

Lisa dashed to her car while I leisurely sauntered to mine.

Before I even got my jeans out of the back seat, Lisa was at my side.

"Here," she said, thrusting a bottle into my hands. I glanced around at all the dark cars. No one was watching. Reluctantly, I took a sip. It didn't taste good. She grabbed it, took a big gulp. She glanced back at the school and mimicked Mr. Monroe: "Give you one minute."

At her insistence, I took a second sip.

"Here's to the king and queen," she said, taking another big drink.

"Strong stuff," I warned.

"You always were cautious," she smiled, slipping the bottle inside the boot she carried.

We went back in. I didn't see much of her (thankfully) the rest of the evening.

Of course, the evening was cut short.

About 10 o'clock I saw Amy dancing with a ninth grader. I didn't like it. She had always stayed with other seventh graders, usually girls. When ninth graders go with seventh graders, it's usually bad news. Two girls in our class dated older guys and ended up pregnant. Rumors had it that several others got pregnant too, but they had had abortions.

The ninth grader was pulling her close and pawing her sides. I felt my anger rise.

At that time Sarah was sitting between Steve and me. Both of them saw it too, saw my reaction.

I stood, began walking resolutely across the floor. What I'd do when I got there, I didn't know.

The music was loud, the air stuffy. Just as I reached them, Amy wilted like a flower. The scruffy ninth grader stepped back and disappeared into the crowd.

I caught Amy as she fainted.

Carrying her to the chairs, I was aware that everyone nearby had stopped dancing and was staring at us.

Mr. Monroe was immediately at my side. "What's wrong?"

"I don't know."

I set her down in the nearest chair and leaned her forward. After a moment, she sat bolt upright, her head flipped back, her eyes opened but couldn't quite focus. I smelled her breath. Mr. Monroe smelled it too.

She was drunk.

"How?" Mr. Monroe shouted angrily.

"I don't know," I snapped back.

We shook her awake and Mr. Monroe pulled her to her feet and led her to the phone. "You know the rules," he said to me.

I nodded.

He called my parents. Amy slumped in a nearby chair. I don't know what their immediate reaction was, but Mr. Monroe listened for awhile, then explained a second time exactly what had happened.

He hung up and turned to me. "According to our policy, your parents have to come and get her. However, since you have the car, you are to take Amy right home. I'll call in a few minutes to make sure you arrive."

I nodded and looked down.

"I know I can trust you," he said, "but we have to follow the rules for everyone."

"I understand," I mumbled.

He put his hand on my shoulder. "I'm sorry your evening was ruined."

I turned to look for Sarah. She was right behind me. "I'm sorry, Sarah," I said.

She smiled, understanding. "You can't help it." She kissed me quickly on the cheek. "The king now has to be a chauffeur. Don't worry about me, I'll get a ride home."

Steve and Aaron also stood nearby, ready to help if needed. "I'll give Sarah a ride," Steve offered.

"Thanks," I said.

Amy was still dizzy and disoriented as we drove home. We had only gone two blocks when she started to retch and I had to pull over. She opened the door and threw up. The vomit steamed in the cold snow.

"You okay?" I asked, not sympathetically.

"I don't know," she muttered and flopped back against the seat. I reached across her and pulled the door shut.

We arrived home. All the lights were on. Mom and Dad rushed to the car as soon as I drove up. They helped get her inside. Mom had been crying, but as soon as she took Amy, she became an effective nurse.

She threw Amy in the shower.

Dad sat down in the living room sofa. He looked pale, acted nervous. I still stood by the door with my coat on, my hands in my pockets.

"Do you know anything else?" he asked.

I shook my head, shrugged. "I don't understand how it happened. Some kids must've slipped booze into the bathroom."

"Who was she with?"

"Different kids. I didn't pay attention until right before she fainted."

Dad erupted. "She's your sister!" He stood, shouted: "You gotta watch out for her."

I lost my temper too and stepped forward. "I do! I was the one who caught her!"

"Don't raise your voice to me!" Dad roared. He stepped nearer and then slapped me across the face, hard. He glared at me and then turned away.

I was momentarily stunned. Tears stung my eyes. My cheek hurt and I was furious. At him. At Amy. I refused to cry.

I spun, stormed out the door, slamming it behind me. I blinked my eyes clear. The moon cast a blue light over the snow and the ice-tipped trees. A slight breeze pushed a few flakes off the roof. They fluttered onto my head, down my neck. The chill felt good. I took several deep breaths.

I stood there a long time.

Later, Mom came out, wearing a coat and hat. "Amy's feeling better," she said, putting her arm around me. She felt warm.

"Good."

"Your dad told me what happened. He's sorry."

"Why doesn't he tell me himself?" I snapped.

She looked down. "He's . . . he's so proud."

"So am I!" I looked at her red eyes, realized her great fatigue, her own sorrow. "I'm sorry, Mom. I don't mean to take it out on you. Let's go inside. It's cold."

As I entered the living room, I took off my coat. Dad sat impassively on the sofa, hands on his knees, jaw set. He could've been a statue. The television was blaring inanely. A talk show host told a joke. The audience, on cue, laughed.

"We can't let our emotions get away from us," he stated.

That was the closest I knew he'd come to an apology. I stared at him, still angry, still confused.

"Tell us again what happened," Mom said, rubbing my arm.

I took a breath and began.

When I'd finished, Amy, wearing her blue bathrobe, wandered in. Her hair was freshly shampooed and piled up in a towel. She put her hands on her hips, looking at each of us in turn.

"Well?" she said defiantly. She expected a lecture.

"How did you feel at the dance?" Mom asked.

She looked away, stared at the TV. "Sick."

"Then you've learned the consequences."

Amy pursed her lips, crossed her arms. I hadn't known that she could be so stubborn. Must run in the family.

"Come," Mom said, patting the sofa beside her. "Sit for a minute."

Amy did, became pale for a moment. She shivered and I thought she was going to throw up again. Mom nodded to me to turn off the TV. I did just as the audience began laughing again.

"Where did you get the alcohol?" Mom asked.

"I'm not gonna rat on my friends," she snapped, hurt and furious and shocked that Mom would ask such a question. Mom's question made sense to me: I also wanted to know.

Silence.

Mom and Dad exchanged worried glances. I could hear the clock ticking in the dining room.

I broke the silence. "Some friends," I quipped.

Amy glared at me, her blue eyes narrowing. Mom and Dad relaxed a bit.

"We'll talk about it tomorrow, when we're not so tired," Mom said, leading her to her room.

I went to my room as well. I heard Mom and Dad talking for awhile, Dad complaining about how he'll have to face the people at school on Monday, Mom crying some more.

I rubbed my cheek. It still stung where Dad hit me. It will for a long time.

Saturday: I am exhausted. In the one-act contest we got third in the region and very glowing comments from the judges. I should be excited along with the rest of the cast, but I feel so emotionally numb, like my soul's been shot with novocaine.

The day began when we loaded the bus at 8 a.m.—I was really dragging—I guess I stayed up too late writing . . .

Thankfully no one mentioned the night before.

Once past Rochester, we line-drilled the rest of the way to Winona. Miss G. looked stunning in her dress suit, winter coat, hat. Mr. Monroe drove the bus. He looked as tired and haggard as I did.

After we arrived and unloaded our set, we walked around the Performing Arts Building. I'd never been to a college before. I was really impressed. Everything seemed new, not old and decrepit like most high school buildings.

The college students showed us through the backstage areas. They had a huge, well-lit makeup room (with adjoining showers!) They also had an immense storage area for props, furniture, and costumes. Imagine what someone could do with that! We couldn't see the stage right away because a play was already in progress. (With the dance the night before, Miss G. wisely thought we should sleep as late as we could.)

We then got into costume and makeup. I'll never get used to that junk.

When we finally got to see the stage—it was huge! Above us were all sorts of ropes and curtains. They had a communication system backstage so they could talk to the light booth. (Later I climbed up there. What a set-up: more dimmers than I could count. From there you could hear the play through small speakers and look out over the entire audience.)

During the performance, I put all my pent up anger at my dad into the part, and my voice sailed across the theater. Later, Miss G. said it was the best I'd ever done. At the time I thought it helped relieve my bitterness and anger. Now, however, when I think about my dad, my cheek still hurts.

I'm too tired to write more except that I'm glad I wasn't home today. While I was at the contest, Pastor Jim called on my family. I'm sure he was as helpful as anyone could be, but it's something Amy and my folks have to work out for themselves.

Sunday: Everyone slept in this morning. Sarah called right after dinner to congratulate me on the play. I also think she wanted to find out how things were going at home. She sure is considerate. As I write and look out my bedroom window, it's a quiet winter afternoon. A soft snow is falling. The phone hasn't rung since Sarah's call. I think we'll all try to blot Friday out of our memories.

Monday: Kids and teachers congratulated us on doing well on Saturday. For me, that day has become a blur. If it wasn't for what I wrote, I don't think I'd remember even that. In school no one said anything about the dance or about Amy. I wonder if it is embarrassment or awkwardness. It surely isn't ignorance. News travels fast in a small town.

Amy (along with Mom and Dad) was called into the office today as part of the "policy." The faculty was pretty supportive of Dad, or so it seemed. He acted a little happier, a little more relieved, at the end of the day than he had been at the beginning. He walked a little straighter, smiled a little broader.

I still wonder—how could Amy cave into peer pressure like that?

"The kids had it in the bathrooms," she told us Sunday. "I just had to go along. I didn't want to lose my friends."

How can you fight such a warped attitude? Those friends will either like her or not—they won't not like her for being herself, not if they're really friends. And if they're not—who cares?

And yet, I can't cast the first stone. I caved in with Lisa. If we hadn't been rushed to get back, would I have stayed with her? Would I have been the one to get sick on the darkened gym floor?

I have to learn from Amy's experience, even if she doesn't. I have to learn to be myself and that has to be good enough.

Tuesday: Melanie and I began work on a two-part editorial on pornography. Mrs. W. suggested the topic to us, a classic confrontation between community standards and free press.

During lunch, Steve heard me talking about it. "I think my folks have some stuff," he said.

"Your folks have pornography?" I joked, knowing that straighter parents than his couldn't be found.

"No," Steve blushed. "On pornography. You know, on the various studies. It came from a Christian family organization. You can borrow it if you like."

He'll bring it tomorrow. I hope I can use some of it.

Also during lunch, Steve and Walter ganged up on me to go to the winter retreat next weekend. I felt pressured and, with my new resolve, declined. Lately, things are just too busy. I need time to myself.

Part of me wondered, though, do I stand up to the right kinds of peer pressure and cave in to the wrong?

I wish I could return to our farm, sit on the hillside. It was always quiet there. As the sun set, I could watch the wind blow across the fields, feel it brush my face. I could think. From that spot, I could see so far.

Wednesday: I was really impressed with the material Steve brought. What they mean by pornography isn't just pictures of naked women but all sorts of bizarre and unnatural things—violent, cruel, and perverted acts. What I read made me nauseated. It's hard to believe that people would think up such things and just as hard to believe that people would pay to see it.

I showed Melanie the material. She turned livid. "It's using people," she said angrily. "Demeaning women and children."

"They view people as animals. No, worse than that. If they treated animals like that, the Humane Society would stop them. The pornographers see people as things."

In a few minutes we had the word processor really humming. For once, Melanie and I were in full agreement.

It's not a problem of community standards vs. free speech, it's a question of mental health and the value of human life. When we finished with part one, Mrs. W. read it.

"Good start," she said, "but begin again."

"Why?" I asked.

"You give too many answers right away. Start with the questions and set the stage. Don't tell the readers what you feel. Convince your audience. If you convince them, then you've made them think what you think, feel what you feel."

Melanie and I will begin again tomorrow.

Thursday: Part one of editorial is done. Mrs. W. stood up from her desk as we handed it to her. She smiled broadly as she read it. "Now this is great writing," she announced, and set it in the "print" file.

Later I saw Amy in the hall surrounded by ninth grade boys. Her hair was fixed up and she wore some new make-up. She's really getting to be attractive, but it bothers me that she's hanging around some real jerks.

I wish I could talk to her about it.

Mom has had some long conversations with her in her room but Amy emerges more defiant than ever while Mom staggers out of those "talks" tired and frustrated.

"I don't know what to do about Amy," she confided in me the other day. "She wants to be popular. She'll do anything to be the center of attention or hide anything that would make her an outcast."

"I never saw this coming in her."

"I did. She's been angry with Dad for a long time, even before we moved. She blames him for losing the farm, blames him for a lot of things."

I don't know where this is all going to end. I'm afraid for Amy. And she's too blind to be scared for herself.

Saturday: After work last night there was no time to write. Everyone's on that retreat—even Sarah was invited and went along. I wish now that I would have gone. It's so quiet around here. Mom and Dad are tense and snap at each other. Dad walked up to school for something but I think he just wanted to be outside for awhile . . . .

Bob Swanson just called. He has a car for sale. He's buying a newer one and wondered if I'd be interested in his old one.

"I can pick you up, bring you out here. You can drive it home, look it over."

He's coming over here now . . . .

I looked over his Monte Carlo and took it out on the highway. It rode so smoothly, it practically glided. I sailed it home. By then, Dad was back, having a cup of coffee in the kitchen.

"No," he stated without even looking at the car.

"You don't even know the price."

Mom and Amy had their coats on and were heading outside to look.

"We can't afford it."

"We can't, but maybe I can."

He was quiet for a second and set his cup down. "What about money for school next year?"

"Almost all of the money I've earned has gone into the bank. If I keep it up, and with what I can make this summer between pizza and working for Mr. Leroy, I'll do fine. Come on," I pleaded. "Just look at the car."

Dad lifted the blinds, stared outside at the car.

He stood up abruptly. "Let's go for a ride."

As it stands now, Dad will float me a no-interest loan so that I won't touch savings and I've promised to reserve that money for college. By next Tuesday I should have a car of my own again.

Wednesday: Life has been really changing around here. I now drive a blue '76 Monte Carlo, the last of the long design. It has some rust on the door bottoms and on the rear and it leaks a little transmission fluid, but it handles well on the highway. Bob now has a two-year old, red T-Bird. He can have the best car in school; I'm just glad I have my own wheels again.

Our editorial came out today. It caused a lot of discussion in school, exactly what an editorial should do, according to Mrs. W.: make people think.

District basketball play-offs have begun for the girls. They might make it to the finals. They won their first game Monday and won again tonight.

Business was slow at Hillcrest Pizza tonight until the game was over and then we were flooded with students coming back into town. After the next game, the kids will stay in Rochester where the finals will be played.

Boys' district playoffs start next Monday. I'm driving "the group" in *my* car.

Thursday: Miss G. nabbed me as I walked into her room today. She wants me to be stage manager for the musical.

"I can't sing."

"I know. But you're responsible."

"I'm too busy. This college prep stuff is tough."

"Good. It's meant to be. But if you're too busy to be stage manager, would you be willing to run the lights? We're buying new cords to put the dimming system out in the audience. You can watch the play as you run lights and use our new headphones to talk to the backstage workers."

"Just like Winona?"

"No, just like the Guthrie," she smiled.

Her smile always gets me—that, and new toys to play with.

Friday: I drove, and Aaron and I saw a movie. Lots of special effects that you don't see in the old movies. Great fun, but I kind of like a story about people, too. After the movie, we hit the loop. We generally made fools of ourselves, and it was great: just like when we were sophomores and juniors.

How long can high school friends stay friends after high school before they drift apart? I know I've wondered that before.

Back to Aaron. He's talking again about his plans to go into business. He has big dreams of fantastic success, of making mountains of money, of owning the best of everything. Is that because his mother doesn't have much? With six kids, she doesn't have much money to go around.

Yet Steve has four brothers and two sisters, and he isn't driven to become rich. He says he'd like to become a missionary. He's been talking lately about going on a short-term mission trip this summer, if he can raise the support.

What's Walter going to do? Though he has a big heart, I know he can't read well. He gets extra help to even pass his high school classes. Maybe he'll work at the Pressboard Company in Maple Valley. His dad's worked there for years.

As for me, I still don't know what I want to do. Maybe I could go into business too, or engineering. But then I don't think I'm good enough in math. I've thought about construction work. Maybe I could be an electrician. I would like a job that's flexible. I don't want to be trapped in a job (like Dad) which isn't my first choice.

Mrs. Webster keeps talking about how jobs of the future will change, that we'll end up changing not just jobs but careers several times during our lives. Who would've thought a few years ago that we would be using word-processing computers instead of typewriters? Look at how we use calculators so much now. The future seems exciting and frightening at the same time.

Mom says she prays for me and for my future each day. I suppose I should pray too, but I don't. I'm afraid to. Afraid to try the real praying that some people do. I don't know if "religion" is for me yet.

Sunday: After Sunday school (Pastor Jim led a discussion based on part 1 of my editorial), Pastor Jim gave me a book to read on the historical basis for the Gospels.

"I've noticed how you like to investigate issues. When you have time, would you like to read this?"

"Okay," I said. The book sits on the floor by my bed. I'm not sure when I'll get around to it.

Monday: Even though I've outgrown the thrill of driving my own car to school, I've been driving anyway. Though I could share a ride with Dad, it's too hard riding with him. We've never talked much, but since the night of Amy's drinking, we talk even less. It's difficult to even look at him without remembering the slap.

I guess I shouldn't worry about our not talking. Most kids seem to have trouble with their parents. (Yet at the same time I know Steve and Sarah don't, and I don't think Walter does.) Aaron's parents are divorced, so he doesn't see his dad very often anyway. Melanie's father's a truck driver so he's gone much of the time, but it sounds as if she argues regularly with her mom. Bob's parents seem to be gone so often that he doesn't see them long enough to fight with them. Cliff's dad's dating (if that's the word) Lisa's mom. I could go on and on. In a small town, there aren't any secrets.

Tuesday: It sounds as if everyone in school auditioned for the musical. I told Miss G. I'd run lights.

I've been working on the yearbook in my free time. I was behind but finally finished the layout for the fall play. Mrs. W. read the copy and set it aside to send to the printer. My goal is to finish the one-act page tomorrow.

The town wants the school newspaper staff to organize (and

write) a special booklet on the 125th anniversary of Hillcrest. Even though she's already too busy with journalism, Mrs. W. agreed to supervise the project. From what I've seen, there are two kinds of teachers: those who are underworked and those who are overworked. Mrs. W. and Miss G. are definitely overworked.

Bob S. has a big party planned. Aaron talked about it and thought we could go together. I think he wanted me to drive. I feel funny about going, but I'll feel left out if I don't. I wish I didn't care.

P.S. Boys' basketball team is still in district playoffs.

Wednesday: Cast list for *The Sound of Music* came out today. Seems as if Miss G. cast every student in the senior high. Terry Williams got the captain part (a surprise choice), Melanie got the part of Maria. I'm glad Amy got a part as one of the kids. She needs something to be involved in and her two-week suspension from activities is over.

Most of the ninth grade burnouts aren't interested in plays, or anything constructive for that matter. This play may keep Amy away from them.

We worked on organizing the 125th in journalism today. Most of us are going to interview some of the old timers. I think I'll interview Grandpa. Even though he's forgotten everything from recent years, he still remembers a lot about his childhood. Hillcrest would have been about 35 years old when he was born. Wow. I never thought about how old he really is.

Aaron's still after me to go to Bob S.'s party next week. I said I'd go. I don't feel right about it, almost as if I ate some food that's upset my stomach.

Thursday: Got home late from BB game. Boys won. Have to get some college prep vocabulary done.

Friday: Worked late and I hardly saw my family today. Mom had a snack of fresh chocolate chip cookies set out for me, so fresh the chocolate was still partly melted. She is so thoughtful.

Life seems easier lately when I don't spend time with my family. Dad and I are both on edge when we're together and Amy gets mad at everyone and everything.

Being gone has its advantages.

Saturday: A day of the unexpected.

A big March blizzard hit during the night, the type of storm that carries the heavy wet snow that weighs down branches and sucks cars right off the road and into the ditch.

Since I couldn't go out, I cleaned my room—a twice a year event. When I finished, the snow had subsided and the plows were out. Mom and Dad decided to brave the conditions and visit Grandpa. I went downstairs and found Amy watching some mindless TV program.

I tried to be friendly. Things have been strained between us for some time. "Do you want to go over your lines?" I asked.

"No," she snapped, flopped back on the sofa and hugged a pillow.

"Just trying to be helpful."

"I don't need any help from you."

A slow, boiling anger rose in me at my lippy punk sister. "Listen," I said, standing over her, "I don't know what your problem is, but it's not my fault you got drunk."

"Oh?" Instantly she sat up, threw her head back, crossed her arms over the pillow. "Who are you to preach?"

I wanted to slap her but remembered Dad. I didn't. "What do you mean by that?" I moved and stood between her and the TV.

"You're the one who was drunk at Swanson's."

Furious, I grabbed her upper arm, hoisting her up. For a split second she looked scared, then she was defiant again. "When?"

"Around Christmas."

"I was not."

"And you went to bed with Lisa Overlund."

I squeezed her arm so hard she hollered.

I spoke firmly and evenly: "I did not."

Her defiant confidence cracked just a bit and she glanced down. "Everyone says so."

"I don't care what everyone says. I didn't get drunk and I barely talked to Lisa."

I forced my anger down, told myself to relax. I released her arm, stepped away. "Sorry. I didn't mean to get mad like that. It's just that, well, it's a lie."

She rubbed her arm. "But you did go to the party?"

"Yes. I was there. I didn't know what to expect. A lot of people were drinking heavily. I didn't. If you want to know everything, I had about a half a can of beer before I left the can somewhere."

"But all the kids said—"

Angered again, I nearly shouted: "I don't care what your friends are saying!"

Sighing, I sat down on the sofa. Anger wasn't getting me anywhere. I struggled to remain calm. "Maybe they're repeating a lie from someone else." I couldn't resist a chance to be big brother. "Or maybe they're lying to get you to do something stupid."

That was a mistake. She flared up again, angrily placing her hands firmly on her hips. "They wouldn't lie to me."

I looked down at the carpet, frustrated. My hands trembled. She wasn't wise enough to know that others lie often and often with little reason.

There was no way to win this argument. I backed down. I shrugged. "Maybe not. But somebody is. That night Lisa was drunk. I brushed her aside. Maybe she confused someone else with me."

Amy suppressed a shudder. "Nobody would be that confused. Not to realize—"

"Do you remember the dance?"

She stared at the TV, blinked several times, slowly. Finally: "No."

Essentially that was the end of our talk. It was good we did, for we cleared the air.

"How about those lines now?" I asked.

She sighed. "Okay," she said sheepishly.

Thursday: I haven't written lately because school and work has kept me busy. Everything's still hectic, but I want to recap the week.

Sunday: We all went to church. It was the first time Amy attended since the dance. She was really worried that people would be snotty. Dad even went to church to provide some moral support. She had no reason to be concerned: people were friendly. No one acted oddly or looked down at Amy or at us.

Monday: I caught up on all my yearbook material and began work on the 125th. I also planned an editorial that I'll write myself. I don't think I could do it with Melanie—more on that later.

Tuesday: The musical is organized and getting blocked and choreographed little by little. This time I can relax and watch the show. Running lights is fun. Boys BB won again. I missed the game and worked. Mr. Richter would have let me off but I'd rather wait until regional play-offs.

Wednesday: Part two of our editorial came out. Everyone thought it was well-reasoned and well-written but many other students thought pornography shouldn't be regulated (as we suggested). It still confuses me. People say porn doesn't affect the mind. In other words, what people see doesn't affect their behavior. Yet advertisers spend millions to make commercials (what people see) which are designed to change spending habits (what people do). Someone is either lying to protect the porn industry, or someone is bilking advertisers out of millions of dollars. Both con games are making lots of money.

Anyway, Melanie and I are satisfied with our work. Maybe that is all that really matters.

Tonight: The big game—district championship. Gotta run—Steve's picking everyone up. I wonder if he'll pick up Sarah first?

Tomorrow's the party. I don't feel good about it but I said I'd go.

Friday: Boys won. Euphoria in school, yet the party (now a victory party) loomed over me like a thundercloud on the horizon.

I picked up Aaron after work and drove out to Bob's. His parents were gone and this time I had my $2 ready.

"Good article," he said, slapping me on the back. "But don't watch the TV."

He didn't see me blush as I headed down the stairs. I felt like a hypocrite.

"Regulated," I said weakly, my back to him. "Not outlawed." I don't know if he even heard me. Or if he cared.

Things only got worse.

Aaron started drinking right away and became a stand-up comic, mimicking various teachers and kids who weren't there. Jennifer came a little while later.

I took a beer that was thrust into my hand, showing my true inability to say no. I didn't drink any: double hypocrite! I placated my conscience without having the guts to stand up for my convictions. I remembered what Amy had heard: How many lies would come out of tonight? In a small town not only are there no secrets but even something that never happened can quickly become fact.

Guilt by association.

Music blared. People laughed at the raunchy video. I looked around. Aaron had wandered off. All around me was chaos, drunkenness, and loud laughter. I was ready to leave. I had no one to talk to; in fact, no one was really talking anyway. I felt tired. I looked for Aaron.

Eventually I found him upstairs in the kitchen. Bob stood awkwardly by the door, looking extremely uncomfortable. Aaron stood very close to Jennifer, both conversing in low tones. He looked worried and she was crying.

I approached Bob, asked what was going on.

He shrugged and sniffed and looked off, awkwardly. "I don't like them up here but I hate to interrupt."

"When they break apart, I'll take him home."

He looked relieved, smiled. "Thanks."

"Call me when I can nab him." Not knowing what else to do, I went downstairs again.

Lisa met me at the bottom of the steps, grabbed my arm, giggled. Her blouse was buttoned wrong. She hastily pulled me into a side room. It was dark.

"The room's clear now," she said softly, and ran her hand along my thigh.

I pushed her away.

"What's the matter?" she said, clutching my arm. "Don't you like me?"

"Of course I do," I replied hastily. "I just don't go to bed with, uh, anybody." I didn't say that I hadn't ever been to bed with anyone and I certainly wouldn't start with her.

"Hey, it's no big deal." She put her arm around my neck. "We just have a fun time, no commitments. You don't have to use anything if you don't really want to. I'm—" she pressed close to me, "safe." She leaned against me, kissed my neck.

I felt myself responding to her. I know it's hard to believe, her half drunk, probably even had someone already that night, but my resolve started to cave in. My pulse raced. I didn't know what to do.

A Bible verse shot into my mind, something the Apostle Paul wrote about "fleeing."

I did just that.

Bob was coming down the stairs. "Take them both home," he said, glad to see me. "They'll be wet blankets on the party. I'll tell Sally that Jen won't go home with her."

He was gone.

I went upstairs, got them. As we came out the door, Melanie and some new guy were strolling up the walk.

"Oh, hi. We're just making an appearance," she said.

"Just making a disappearance," I quipped. I'm not sure what she thought, but her boyfriend looked disdainfully at me. Who cares?

Aaron and Jennifer rode in the back seat. I drove to her home first. They kissed a long time in the back seat. She cried some more. He saw her to the door. They kissed some more.

When I dropped him off, he explained.

"She's pregnant."

Saturday: I didn't sleep well last night, worrying about Aaron and Jennifer. All their options are difficult and full of unanswerable questions.

I thought quite a bit about what I would do in his situation yet I'm sure that it wouldn't happen to me. But maybe all kids think that, that I'm somehow invulnerable, indestructible. Maybe Aaron and Jennifer had once thought that.

Part of me says that since they made their bed (literally), they have to lie in it. It was their choice and they must face the consequences. Sadly, though, Jennifer could—and might—get an abortion. That's the "easy" solution, yet the baby has no choice, has no say. And how will she handle the guilt?

Pregnancy isn't accidental and I suppose it isn't always premeditated. Abortion is.

If she chooses to keep the baby, that changes her life plans. Would Aaron feel obligated to marry her? Would it be out of love? Even if he does love her, when problems arise, would he wonder more if he did indeed love her? Would he resent the pressure that had been placed on him? If he doesn't marry her, he should be obligated to pay child support payments—but would he?

What if she gave the baby up for adoption? Would she always wonder about its future? At least, though, the child would have a future, whereas abortion kills all possibilities.

The choice is Jennifer's, and Aaron can only wait until she decides.

I hate to consider this possibility, but I wonder if she wanted to get pregnant. A baby hooks him.

Sunday: What a coincidence! Sunday school's topic was abortion. Everyone had strong opinions but few of us had real information. A lot of the kids started their comments with "I heard that—" or "What if—?" We all gave fictional or hypothetical situations.

What about real persons facing real problems?

It's not easy.

Pastor Jim had a lot of data and Bible verses. Since he is against abortion, he paints it black and white. As for me, I have some questions on both sides. If churches come out and say abortion is murder, are they willing to help pregnant girls?

If a baby isn't human until it's born (as pro-choicers must think) what about a premature baby? Isn't it human? What makes a child "human" the moment it is born? Wasn't it the same a few minutes before? A few days before? A few months?

I don't buy the argument about a woman having a right over her own body, not if another human being is involved, and that human being is in her body. Yes, a woman has rights over her own body, but hasn't a woman abdicated that right a bit when she decides to have sex? Babies are a natural consequence after all.

What about the father? How come he gets off scot-free? Isn't he responsible for the child that's born? But the way I understand it, even if he wanted the child born, he can't stop an abortion.

If we as human beings have a complete right to do what we want with our own bodies, how come drugs (a form of self-destruction) are illegal? Yet abortion (nothing less than baby-destruction) isn't.

It sure seems like the laws are all messed up.

Thursday: Time is rushing fast. My senior year is almost three-quarters over.

Boys' basketball lost tonight. Everyone was depressed afterwards but I'm sure they'll rebound (no pun intended) by Friday. I've seen it happen before.

I've been busy with work and writing my college prep paper on *Lord of the Flies.* It sure was a hard book to get into but by the third chapter it picked up. The way Miss G. explains it, Piggy represents the Superego, Ralph the Ego and Jack the Id. My paper analyzes the symbolic aspect of their characters.

It's getting late. I've gotta re-read some more.

Friday: Changed my *Lord of the Flies* topic last night. Deadline is Wednesday so I have to get it done this weekend if at all possible.

All the characters are either reduced to or destroyed by savages. The author Golding is saying that we're all savages underneath and it's society that holds back "The Lord of the Flies."

I called Pastor Jim tonight and he gave me some Bible verses to tie in. He was really helpful and wanted to read the paper when I'm done. (Maybe I can get him to proofread it for me? I wonder if he can spot spelling errors?)

Later—

I got behind on my paper because Aaron stopped over. I tried to keep any advice to myself. I have enough trouble solving my own problems—why work on his?

Besides, if he doesn't like my advice, he won't take it. If he does, he'll follow it and blame me afterwards. I've seen Dad do that with Mom lots of times.

Well, back to *L. of the F.*

Saturday: Finished! I'll type it into the word processor on Monday. Maybe Mrs. Webster will give me a pass from study hall.

Miss G. has a set crew work time today. Amy and I are heading over to school now . . . .

Later—

Worked on the captain's house. Another staircase!

Amy was pretty good at painting the flats. I think she admires Miss G. That's a good thing. Young kids need quality teachers to look up to.

Since our talk, Amy and I get along pretty well together, maybe the best we ever have. Both of us share a common frustration with Dad—sad that we have something like that to talk about.

Sunday: I read a little of Pastor Jim's book last night and fell asleep. When I awoke I didn't feel like Sunday school, but I did make it to church.

We visited Grandpa in the afternoon. The nursing home was quiet today. There weren't many other visitors. Lots of the residents just shuffled up and down the halls. We found Grandpa, as usual, sitting in his vinyl easy chair. He was watching his small black and white television.

I asked him if he'd let me interview him for the 125th anniversary project. He scratched his chin and seemed pleased.

My challenge will be that once I get him talking, how will I get him to stop?

Monday: Paper done. Gave it to Pastor Jim after school. Began writing my editorial. I'm going to combine it with my last term paper—Hillcrest teenage attitudes on sex—and kill two birds with one topic.

Next week I'll interview a bunch of kids and promise them anonymity. Maybe I'll design a survey for the term paper. Of course, many kids lie on surveys. Some try to shock and some need to hide the truth.

Lots of tests coming up this week. End of the quarter Friday.

Tuesday: Jennifer showed off her engagement ring today in school. She'll be the first senior to be married. The girls seemed (acted?) impressed, and the guys didn't care.

I felt bad that Aaron didn't tell me earlier, that I had to see the ring myself. I wonder how they'll afford the ring, what with the wedding and the baby on the way.

(What if she miscarries? Would Aaron end the engagement?)

"Do you love her?" I had asked him just last week. He was sitting in my room, depressed, hanging his head.

For an answer, he shrugged, looked off. "I guess so."

What do any of us know about love? The songs sing about it, but if you separate sex and lust from the word "love," song lyrics would be wiped out.

First of the big tests tomorrow. I better review.

Thursday: I worked late Wednesday and have been dragging all day. I staggered through my college prep test, guessing more than I should have. I couldn't remember the difference between a participle and a gerund. Fortunately, part two of the test (tomorrow) will be an essay. I should do fine. I can usually find the words to say something.

After school I drove over to see Grandpa. The nursing home, though clean, always has a strong pungent smell—is it from all the catheters or is it from chemicals used to cover up other odors? Anyway, where Grandpa is, each resident has his own small apartment. Most of the residents congregate around the TV areas. Many of them are wheeled in. Grandpa, though, when he leaves his room can usually be found with two other residents playing pool in the recreation room. They also have a Ping-Pong table there but no over ever uses it.

Grandpa's aging quickly now. His skin is getting loose and saggy around his neck. His nose seems to stick out more and his eyes water constantly. His hair is mostly gone and his warped, arthritic hands are covered with age spots.

I brought my tape recorder. My fears came true: once I got him talking, I couldn't get him to stop. He told me all about Josephine the telephone operator, the horses on Main Street, the old cattle business, Adam Brothers' Woodworking, and the creamery that burned in 1947. It's amazing when I realize how much Hillcrest has changed during his lifetime, and how much more (according to Mrs. Webster) our society will change during mine.

Grandpa, fortunately, was in one of his rare lucid moods

when he not only remembered the distant past clearly, but he also recalled last week.

Suddenly, though, he launched into a sermon.

"Throughout history," Grandpa said, "people don't change. They're always worried about tomorrow's paycheck, worried about the person they'll marry, worried whether enough rain will fall next spring. People complain about their homes, their families, their health, but never complain about themselves, their real selves."

He adjusted himself in his vinyl easy chair and it let out a squeaking groan. He leaned toward me. "When was the last time I complained about my knee?"

"When I first came," I smiled.

He raised a bushy eyebrow. "Oh. That recent? Well, see what I mean? But when was the last time I complained about my stubbornness?"

"Uh, never, I guess."

"Never is right. Take Mrs. Henderson down the hall. She's always complaining about her family, but does she ever complain about her own constant whining? Or George next door?" He lowered his voice. "He complains about his eyesight but never about his own gossip."

Grandpa patted my knee. "I see this only now, at age ninety, when my knee's bad, my bladder weak, and I eat more pills than real food. Chad, learn it earlier than that. Take time to look at yourself. You won't be so quick to complain about anything, or anyone, else."

I nodded, not sure what he was getting at but knowing that old people want their listeners to agree with them.

I wanted to return to his memories. "What do you remember about my parents when they were young?"

He leaned back, rubbed his chin. "Your grandmother and I were sure proud of your dad when he was little." He began a long story about my grandmother, then about his brothers who both died young. He finally talked about my parents. "Your mom was the best catch in the county. Your father met her at a high school game in Paradise. A real sweetheart then and still is. Not many good people come out of that town, but she was one of them. I'm always telling the nurses about her."

I set down my notes, closed my book, and turned off the recorder. He rambled on. I had all I needed for the 125th special. We weren't going to write about family histories.

He suddenly grew perturbed and shook his head, agitated. "Your father was too bullheaded, like me, but after your mother lost the baby, he was never the same."

My heart skipped a beat. "What?"

"When that baby died, Charles became depressed, then turned surly," he said, his hand rubbing his chin thoughtfully.

"What baby?" I asked. He didn't hear me.

"Quit going to church. Took it harder than he should have. At first I thought it was because the baby had been another boy, but something deeper was getting to him."

"How old was I then?"

"I don't know. Wait. I remember that Amy was still in diapers because I had to change a really messy one. The baby who died was their third child and their last. The doctors saw to that."

Grandpa told me other details about my parents, about how Dad began working constantly on the farm after Grandpa had sold the land to him.

But I kept wondering about that baby. Why did my parents never mention it? I do vaguely remember Mom being in the hospital once. Her miscarriage had probably happened at that time. I wonder what other secrets they have. Do I really know them?

Friday: Phew! End of quarter.

The last big tests for awhile.

This is the last quarter, then graduation. School's flown by! When I was in seventh grade, graduation seemed an eternity away.

How things change.

Saturday: A nice spring day. The snow cover is completely gone.

No more ice chunks remain under the trees. Tulips are popping up through the soil and the grass is turning green. The weather was so nice today that I washed and waxed Monty. I worked on touching up a few rust spots. It looks better, but I know the rust will only return.

Amy got her bike out and I adjusted the seat for her. Some of those ninth graders have their farm permits and have been driving around our house after school. (They throw a wrench in the back seat and drive to school. Afterwards they show off around town. I guess I'm envious. When I was that age, Dad wouldn't let me drive to school with a farm permit—not until I could get my real license.) I still see her talking to some of those jerks.

In the evening Steve and Walter came over and we drove to Rochester. We went to a movie, walked around the mall, then drove around a bit. I like Steve but sometimes it's hard being with Walter. He says things that don't follow the conversation and then I don't know what to say. I've seen him try hard to fit in with other kids, but the harder he tries, the more obvious it is and the more others avoid him.

If it's a nice day tomorrow we're going to get a group together for softball.

Sunday: Another unusually warm day. We played softball on the tiled field. Steve had invited Sarah. I was glad she was there and on my team. She hits the ball well and looked good on the field. She had her dark hair pulled back in a ponytail. I hadn't noticed it before but she is growing her hair even longer.

I've finally faced reality and given up on Melanie. I can only hope for so long that she'll see me as more than a "friend." I think I have finally ripped her out of my heart.

After the game I had a long talk with Steve. We sat on our car hoods by the field. He's always been quiet—until this year. I guess I was too. Maybe being a senior does something to a person. We realize that we're not protected by parents or school or anything else. We have to make our own decisions. We have to talk, to choose, to act for ourselves.

I told him I sent my test scores to the University of Minnesota and was thinking of engineering.

"I've been accepted into Bethel College."

"Great," I said. I was jealous. How nice, I thought, to know where you're going.

"I don't think the mission field will work this summer. But Pastor Jim says I should start preparing for next summer."

"Sounds like good advice."

"What about you? Have you been praying about your future?"

I looked down, shifted my feet on the bumper. "I don't know." The sun shone on the chrome.

"You know what the Bible says."

"I know. I accept that Christ died and rose but I can't really believe that He wants me to follow him, that I'm worth something, or that He wants the best for me."

"Are you afraid of God? Is that it?"

"Maybe. Or maybe I want to work things out for myself."

"Afraid to really surrender everything to the Lord?"

"Maybe."

"Afraid what the Lord might ask you to do?"

"Maybe." I felt extremely uncomfortable. Hot. It could've been the sun, but I doubt it.

Steve ran his hands along his jeans as if he, too, were nervous. "Even though I've committed my life to Christ, I'm afraid. When I think of the future, sometimes I'm terrified."

I couldn't believe, of all people, that he had said that.

"I'm afraid to be a missionary. I'm afraid of hardship. Of facing the challenges. Of explaining my work to others. But I try to think about how Christ loved me enough to suffer for my sins and die in my place. Since the Lord loves me that much, He'll take care of me. I don't know how I could handle the future without Christ. As a Christian all my problems aren't solved, but the Lord will see me through the problems to the solutions."

I stared stupidly at Steve. Half of me was in awe, the other half was shocked because I had never heard him talk so long at one time. Maybe a missionary's heart beat in him after all.

I shifted on the hood, uncomfortable by the abrupt silence. "I know we're told God loves us, but I've often wondered what love really is."

He looked off, toward the white clouds for a minute. "I think love is giving for someone else. But it's always tied up with commitment." He scratched his neck and seemed to be searching for the words. "Christ made a commitment to us when He went to the cross. The price He paid showed His love. And we show our love for Christ if we really accept his sacrifice, if we really commit ourselves to following Him. Like human love—if there's no commitment to the other person, there's no love. Instead, it's just 'What can I get out of this relationship?'"

We talked longer, but I didn't really listen nor were my comments very meaningful. I had found the answer to my question about love. Without commitment, what looked like love was less than love. A person has to commit to the other person. Totally. For life. As Mom and Dad did.

Even with their present problems, they are still committed to each other. I don't think that will ever change.

Their commitment outweighs any problems that come along.

*   *   *

SECOND SEMESTER, SECOND QUARTER

Wednesday: No time to write but record this: straight A's.
Who would've ever thought it?
Amazing.

Thursday: Another busy week (also raining most of the time)
means little time to write. The new quarter is off to a hectic start.
College prep has become English lit (puke!), and we start with
Beowulf. Why can't they write in normal sentences and
paragraphs? Why did they want to use kennings and alliteration?

I visited Grandpa again tonight. I've been thinking about
Steve's comments about commitment and what Grandpa had
said about Grandma. I asked him about her.

He blinked rapidly and glanced away, suddenly growing
tearful. "She got more beautiful the older she got."

He turned to the framed black and white pictures behind
him on the dresser and pulled several off. "Here she is on our
wedding day. This one is at our farm; look, that's your dad, just
after his fourth birthday."

In the second picture my grandmother looked far older and
more tired. She had taken on the plump, round-shouldered look
that I knew from other pictures.

Grandpa looked longingly, tenderly at the black and white
photographs, then sighed and pursed his lips. Did he see things I
didn't?

Or did he appreciate things I couldn't?

"She was awfully sick around the time of this next picture."

He frowned. "She never got to see your folks married." Grandpa choked up. "It was hard when she was sick. I tried to keep her comfortable, tried to keep the farm going. Fortunately your father was old enough to take over most of the work."

He slowly and tenderly returned each picture to its place, then turned to me. "He lost the farm, didn't he?"

I nodded.

"He's never forgiven himself for that."

"He blames God."

Grandpa nodded in an all-knowing way. "If he blames someone else, he doesn't have to blame himself. He doesn't have to face himself."

Thinking back over our conversation, I've come to the conclusion that Grandpa, even with his fragmented memory, is the wisest man alive.

Friday: I am finally caught up on my yearbook assignments and I've begun planning my editorial. Mrs. W. knows I'm working on something, but she isn't prying. I think she'd like me to experiment.

Sarah and I are going out Saturday, walk around the mall, maybe go to a movie, get some ice cream.

(Maybe I should interview her to begin with? I'm going to be nervous about it anyway. She wouldn't mind.)

We had a special Friday rehearsal tonight where we hit the solo songs and prelim tech work. Mr. Richter said I could leave work early to help Miss G. Sometimes I can't believe how much importance he puts in all school activities, especially the plays.

The lighting for this production will be interesting: lots of scenes and light changes. I think I have all the cues written down but only another rehearsal will tell. The thunder scene is going to be the best.

I must remember what Miss G. says: Do it right, no one notices. Do it wrong and everyone knows.

Saturday: I can talk easily with Sarah. When we had ice cream at the mall, I explained my editorial. In the booths, we were hidden from others but I still felt myself blushing at times.

"Your topic is premarital sex?" she asked, surprised. After her initial shock, she smiled and leaned closer across the table. "Does Mom know?"

"I think she suspects something." I dramatically whipped out my small notebook and pen. "Well?"

She leaned back and deliberately crossed her arms authoritatively. She deepened her voice and pronounced like a minister: "I think sex before marriage is wrong. If people love each other, they should wait until marriage."

"Always?"

"Always." She leaned forward and ran her fingers over her placemat. She dropped her authoritarian act. "Of course, you know I'm a Christian and that's the way I've been taught, but it is common sense too, even apart from the Bible."

"How so?"

"Well, I've heard several girls say that they're pressured from their boyfriends. The 'If you really love me, you'll let me' line. But if the guy really loved her, he wouldn't ask. He'd respect her feelings and her conscience. He wouldn't put his own desires over her feelings."

She then dropped her voice, almost to a whisper, and blushed a little: "One of the girls on our volleyball team gave in to her boyfriend. She said it was nothing like the movies, nothing like the songs. It was horrible, but she got through it, for him. Afterwards he never called her again. Now tell me, was he in love?"

I looked down. The answer was obvious.

I asked: "Was she in love?"

"Maybe. But she was stupid enough to believe that the guy 'had to have it.'"

"Can I quote you?"

She leaned back. "Sure. But if you use that example, change the team. No. On second thought, better not. Readers will find someone to fit the story. Just drop that part. Quote my opinions, not the example."

"Okay," I said.

Too bad. I thought it would have made a good opening.

Later, I didn't know if I should try for a good night kiss, but I'm glad I did. I was nervous about it because we've been good friends lately . . . oh, well, the kiss didn't feel like "friends."

Sunday: In Sunday school today we moved our folding chairs into a circle. We discussed the gray areas, as Pastor Jim calls them—smoking, social drinking, dances, and so forth. Personally, I think they're gray mostly to older people and those raised in strict homes. The rest of the world doesn't see anything questionable about them. I almost said as much in class, but Mary Arnold spoke up first.

Dressed in an attractive spring pink dress, she sat across from me, looking very prim. "I think anything questionable should be avoided," she stated with great finality.

I was stunned. I had seen her guzzling beer at Bob's. Rumor has it she's been around with several different guys. (Of course, rumors can be very wrong—as I well know!) However, she, like me, was at a party that was, by Pastor Jim's standards, very "questionable."

What a hypocrite. It seems churches are havens for the best people (like Steve and the Websters) and the worst hypocrites (like Mary.) But then, maybe she's thinking the same thing about me . . . .

Monday: I showed Mrs. W. my article plan as well as my survey questions. As she read, her eyes widened. She pursed her lips. Nearing the end, she grew excited. "Chad, this is great."

I felt more than good; I felt as if I were accomplishing

something original, something important. She then helped me rewrite several questions so as not to prejudice the answer.

Later in the day she caught me between classes. Students filed by behind me as she explained: "I've made copies and have permission for your survey to be given to the seniors in the industrial arts classes and Miss Gunderson's college prep. The younger students will take their survey in Mr. Monroe's eighth grade math. I'll also give it to my sophomores. We'll hit grades 8, 10, and 12. I should get the results to you by the end of school, Tuesday."

During play practice I interviewed the cast (those that wanted to be) between scenes. I was surprised by the wide spectrum of answers, everything from "a virgin until married" to "it's just something you do on a date. No big deal."

Bob Swanson, however, after I promised complete anonymity, spoke the most explicitly. "As host to some of the best parties in Ironwood County, I know from experience that many kids do it. As for me personally, I've been with many girls since, oh, I don't know, about eighth grade. But then I started dating early." He smiled, rather pleased with himself.

I probed further, knowing he'd rarely had a steady girl friend. I asked him about it.

"Oh, I like to check out different girls. If they show any interest in me, well, I can't be rude, can I?" He laughed.

"Do your parents know about your parties?"

"I sometimes wonder if they guess, but they don't dare ask." He smirked. "But if they asked, they might find out! These girls' parents are the same way—they really don't care if their daughters go to bed or not. All they're worried about is potential babies. 'Don't do it,' they tell them, 'but if you do, take precautions.' Now, if that isn't a green light, I don't know what is."

"If you got a girl pregnant, would you marry her?"

"Why? It's her problem."

I scribbled his answers as quickly as I could.

"What kind of girl would you marry?"

"Oh, I don't know, but she'd have to have a sense of humor, have great knockers, and be a virgin."

"A virgin?"

"Hey, I don't want used merchandise." He laughed crudely and raised his eyebrows knowingly.

I was puzzled by his double standard. "What about all these girls you've been with? What do you think of them?"

"Nice girls. Fun to be with."

"What about someone like Lisa?" I asked.

"Oh. She goes to bed with any guy just to be popular. She's a whore."

"If I use no names, can I quote that?"

He shrugged, "Sure, I don't care."

Thinking back now, I don't know how I was so naive. Maybe I just wanted to be naive. I've always wanted to believe the best about people. Growing up on the farm, sex was never a secret, but my parents strongly taught me that sex only belonged within the bounds of marriage. I assumed that most people believed that. When I think of Aaron and Jennifer, even though she's pregnant, I can't really imagine him going to bed with her.

I'm going to try to interview Lisa tomorrow.

Tuesday: 7:00 P.M. I'm writing this at work. No one's here now, so I thought I'd jot this down before I forget the details of my interview of Lisa:

I found neither time nor place to talk to Lisa during school so I asked her if she'd meet me right after school in the journalism room.

She showed up, excited and bubbly. She sat next to me, sliding her chair closer.

"Everyone's talking about the article you're writing. We all figured the survey had to do with it too."

(So much for a surprise when it's printed!)

I explained what I was doing. She wasn't shy about anything we discussed, although I think I blushed several times. What helped during all these interviews was my acting experience. I imagined myself as Dan Rather doing an interview.

Two highlights: "Guys need it," she said, and really believed it. (She said I could use that.) "One guy I was with was so rough I had to go to the doctor afterwards. (She said I couldn't use that.)

"Do you think guys appreciate . . . you know?"

She leaned back, laughing, and pushed my arm. "It's not like I know many, Chad. But it's expected at parties. It's just something you do. It's no big deal."

"What about your future? What sort of person would you marry?"

For the first and only time, she hesitated and blushed. "I don't know, but someone caring, sensitive, honest, a sense of humor." She then added softly, practically a whisper: "Someone like you."

I laughed off my embarrassment. "Oh, sure!"

She hesitated just a second, then laughed too.

I felt really sorry for her. Bob called her a whore. In her own way, she is as naive as I am.

I don't know what to think, but I recall what Steve said about commitment, how it always goes with love.

What he said makes sense.

Just then Mrs. W. walked into the room and brought the completed surveys. Lisa looked a little uncomfortable. I was late for work. I grabbed the surveys, thanked Lisa, and dashed off.

10:30 p.m.: Looking at the surveys, I'm amazed. Once I discard the jokers (kids who obviously put down funny or impossible answers) only a few points emerge. It seems as if many (but not most) kids are sexually active, but few think about the consequences. Those who are sexually active don't use (or don't want to use) birth control. They don't think they can get pregnant. They have no fear of VD. No one seems to know much about this new thing, AIDS, but it seems deadly. Students don't think it could ever possibly affect them.

Better put this aside. I'm behind on *The Canterbury Tales*. Chaucer was certainly aware of many different attitudes about sex. Pastor Jim once remarked that sex was as old as the human race. I recall the class laughing, as he had expected. It's part of our past, he asked, but how are we going to let it shape our future?

Wednesday: Still working on the article.

Thursday: My article's done and I'm proud of it. I know it's good, but I don't like the notoriety it's brought me. Everyone's asked about the survey results. Even Melanie has been snooping around my table the last few days.

Maybe now she'll see me as someone more interesting. Maybe I should have interviewed her but, to be honest, I was afraid to.

Afraid to talk to her bluntly.

Afraid what she might tell me.

It's late. Test tomorrow.

Friday: Busy night with pizzas.

Mrs. W. said my article was superb, one of the best researched and written in years!

I don't know when I've felt so good about something I've done—

Just got a call from Steve. Walter was in a car accident and was taken to Rochester. He is fine but the car was totaled. Steve didn't have any more information.

Steve and I are going to visit him in the hospital tomorrow. What could've happened?

Saturday: Steve and I just got back from Rochester. From talking to some people last night and Walter this morning, we've pieced the story together.

Our school, like all schools, has a "class" system, a class of jocks and popular kids on top, then a lower class, the kids who don't make the cut (wherever that is). As a former "Aggie" who took agriculture and shop classes, I have a lot of friends in the lower echelon. Walter falls into that group.

It seems that one of the Friday night parties had a lot of drinking. Drugs, too. Walter went, driving his dad's car. He drank some, maybe quite a bit. On the way home, he hit the ditch and flipped the car.

When Steve and I reached the hospital floor, Walter's parents were sitting on a bench in the hall outside the room, conversing quietly. They looked exhausted. They're my parents' ages, yet they looked almost twice as old. They must've been at the hospital all night. His mother told us to go in; he was awake.

Entering Walter's room, we found him propped up in bed, his forehead bandaged and his arm in a cast. He saw us, smiled at first, then glanced away and stared at the stand by his bed.

At first we talked about superficial things, then Walter, staring at his cast, explained in a quivering voice.

"I was at a party." His chin trembled. He was close to tears. "I don't remember much."

Steve touched Walter's shoulder, nodded, seemed close to tears too. I marveled at Steve's compassion. I'll never cease to be surprised by him. I slowly sat on the chair near the bed.

"Pastor Jim came here last night." Walter looked out the hospital window at the dark brick wall across the street. "I'm so ashamed. Everyone knows."

"We all make mistakes," Steve said.

"Everything is so confusing and mixed-up. I remember drinking, but someone must've put something in my drink and I—" He stopped, swallowed, didn't continue.

Steve waited. He said no more.

"You'll feel better when you get home," Steve said optimistically, sitting on the side of the bed.

"Yeah," Walter muttered, not believing it.

Sitting in a chair by the wall, I felt like a useless piece of baggage.

Then Pastor Jim walked in. Steve and I quickly made room for him, standing and moving over to the windows. Walter wouldn't look at him.

"How are you feeling today?"

"Better."

"Just talked to your folks outside. A few more tests, then you'll get to go home tomorrow."

"Great," he said bitterly.

"What's wrong?" Pastor Jim asked.

"How can I face everyone?"

Long silence.

Pastor Jim cleared his throat: "If we were perfect, the cross wouldn't have been necessary."

For the first time, Walter looked directly at him, almost defiantly. "You don't know everything."

"I don't need to," Pastor Jim said calmly and patted his leg. "The Lord does. Christ died once for all. We're just glad you're still with us."

Walter covered his face with his free hand and Pastor Jim sat beside him. Walter sobbed.

Steve and I quietly withdrew into the hall. Walter's father, a quiet, balding man, shook our hands vigorously. "Thanks for coming," he said earnestly. "We're so glad Walter has friends like you."

I didn't deserve any thanks.

Sunday: I cleaned Monty at the car wash today. As I backed out of the car wash stall, three guys were waiting, standing to the side of a muddy pickup—Joe Borlund's. Joe: blond, stocky, crew cut, always sticks out his chest when he walks.

"Hey, Chad, come see this picture!"

I stopped my car, got out, and walked over. They were huddled around an instamatic-photo of Friday's party, laughing. Walter, looking dazed, lay in bed with Karen Olson, the principal's daughter. A blanket was pulled over them so only their faces showed. She looked as dazed as he.

I lunged for the picture, missed.

"Hey!" Joe pushed me back, hard. "It's a great picture."

Without thinking, I hit him. He fell back against the pickup, more in surprise than pain, and dropped the picture to the gravel. I snatched it up, stuffing it into my pocket. The other two guys just stood there, blandly observing the whole thing. Joe stood up and rubbed his chin.

I stormed over to Monty and quickly drove off.

Only now am I finally cooling down. I burned the picture. Kids are mean.

Monday: In the morning, Mrs. W. called me out of sociology class. As I entered her room I saw that she was distraught. She was tapping her pencil on her desk. She nodded to the chair beside her desk. I sat.

Her hands were trembling and she looked close to tears.

"I'm so angry," she began.

"What's wrong?" I had never seen her upset before.

"Mr. Olson is censoring your article."

My face flushed. "He can't do that!"

"He can. He did." She continued to tap her pencil angrily.

"Don't we have the freedom to write what we want?"

Tap. Tap. "Yes. But not publish what we want." Tap. "Every so often he checks our layout, usually once in the fall to 'officially' review our paper." Tap. Her voice grew sarcastic. "To assert his authority."

"Why now?"

"I assume he heard about the survey. Maybe some parent complained. A few always want to keep their heads stuck in the sand."

She paused. "I'm sorry. I shouldn't be talking this way to you, but I'm so angry." She looked away, her jaw set. "It's a good article. An important article. I must respect his authority, but I wanted you to know that I also respect your integrity as a writer."

I stood, determined. "May I have a pass to the office?" She stared at me for a moment, uncertain.

In a few minutes I stood in Mr. Olson's office, a rather stuffy blue room with papers piled high along the left wall and various diplomas and certificates hanging on the right. I faced his desk; the windows were at his back, the track field beyond.

He sat down with a pompous, authoritarian, snorting exhale of air. He ran a hand through his dark, Grecian-formula hair. I never cared one way or another about him but now his every gesture infuriated me. He gestured for me to sit down. I did.

"I've heard good things about you, Chad. Your teachers tell me how your grades have soared."

"Thank you, Mr. Olson. But don't patronize me." (Was I glad for the vocabulary work in college prep!) "You censored my article."

He folded his hands on his desk, cleared his throat. "Not censored, just advised a rewrite."

"So we're free to ignore your advice?"

His hands tensed, his knuckles whitening. "The article, though well-written, gives a bad view of the school and of the student body."

"How so?"

Sighing dramatically, he reached into his desk drawer, pulling out a photocopy of my typeset article. "For example, look at this part about a girl who agrees to go to bed with boys because she wants to feel accepted."

"That's what I was told."

"Hearsay."

"I used no names to protect students, but there's bound to be hearsay in any article like this. It's about students' attitudes on sex."

"And it presents the view that health classes aren't doing their job."

"I don't say that."

"That's how it'll be taken."

"Lots of kids who are having sex aren't using birth control. Personally, I don't think that's something health classes can teach. But if that's the fault of health classes, you're drawing your own conclusion. All I've presented are the prevalent attitudes. Some boys in our school view girls as things to satisfy them. Some girls also see themselves that way. Isn't that important?"

He slid the article back into his drawer. "People don't want to read that students are sexually active."

"People?"

"Parents."

I almost blurted out that maybe he should start looking around as a parent. After all, it was his daughter Karen who had been in the picture with Walter. I didn't bring that up. He would have just gotten angrier and not believed me.

Instead, I recalled Mrs. W.'s phrase. "You're sticking your head in the sand." I stood, smiling politely, adding respectfully: "Mr. Olson."

I left, vowing that the article would be seen, one way or another.

Within a short time the school's gossip telegraph began clicking like crazy. Some teachers (I know it wasn't Mrs. W.) leaked the story to the students who ably carried my indignation.

At suppertime, Dad brought up the subject. His sources had told him that I had been rude to the principal.

"Is it important to be honest?" I responded.

He hesitated, then cautiously replied. "Yes."

"Mr. Olson censored an honest story. I wasn't rude. I just didn't agree with him."

Dad deliberated a moment, frowned, then nodded. He didn't say anything more about it.

Tuesday: The school's gossip lines burned with a new story today. Karen Olson was late for school. When Mr. Olson drove home to find her, he discovered her in the bathroom, unconscious. She had slit her wrists. Fortunately, she had not been successful, for we received word by noon that she was okay and under observation in the hospital.

After school I visited Walter at his home. As I entered his family's small and poorly furnished living room, he turned off the TV. I sat by him. The sofa squeaked. The bandage was off his head and he had combed his hair forward to hide the stitches. He would be in school tomorrow, he said.

"Did you hear about Karen?" he asked, staring at the dark TV.

"Sure, everyone did."

"I feel terrible. Something happened the night of that party. Actually, nothing happened at all, but everyone thinks that it did. A picture—"

I interrupted him: "I saw a picture. One of those instamatics without negatives. The ashes are probably still in my wastebasket."

Walter blinked several times, still staring at the blank TV. Slowly, as he understood, he turned to me and smiled. "No picture any more?"

"Just ashes."

"I'm going to call Karen." Excited, he stood quickly, then looked at me. "Chad, nothing happened. Really."

I stood beside him and touched his shoulder as I had seen Steve do. "I believed you the first time."

I was late for work, but losing some pay was worth it.

Wednesday: Karen and Walter were both in school today. I was surprised she came, but maybe her dad made her, bandaged wrists and all.

The gossip lines dropped the suicide story and picked up my censored article again, fueled by the fact that we had no *Hillcrest Gazette* today.

"—in order to print a double issue highlighting spring sports and next week's musical," Mrs. W. announced over the PA system.

A polite lie, I thought.

In journalism she told me what was happening behind the scenes. The school board caught wind of the article, probably through some talkative kids, and was "working on it."

In other words, they wanted to see for themselves what the article said while allowing Mr. Olson some time to save face.

What a crazy world. Politics instead of education—and the musical next week!

Thursday: In between *Macbeth* (The play improved after Miss G. explained it), yearbook duties, chemistry labs, sociology experiments, and trig, I've spied school board members filing in and out of the principal's office. The superintendent met with Mr. Olson for an hour or so. The gossip mill really churned. Mrs. W. was called into the office late in the day (Steve told me) and the speculations ran like calves let loose from the pasture.

I'm trying to remain calm about the whole thing. After my initial indignation I've tried to have a justice-will-out philosophy (kind of like Shakespeare).

Play practice went well tonight. This was the first time I ran the lights straight through the musical. I hadn't seen the entire play in order before—it's quite different from the movie version and in some ways better.

I hadn't thought of Bob S. being a good cynic before, but now I see that he fits the part well (or the part fits him). Of course, it's hard to keep my eyes off Melanie.

I need an article on the musical for tomorrow's deadline, so I'd best get to it.

Friday: Mrs. W. called me out of class again and told me that my survey article will run next week.

"Oh, and will your musical article be ready today?"

"No problem," I smiled. "All I have to do is type it up."

While typing on the computer, I talked to Melanie who was working beside me. She was extremely friendly.

"I finally read your article," she said. "It's quite good. Mrs. Webster has it all set up in her side office, ready to add this week's extras (here she imitated Mrs. W.) 'Spring sports and musical'."

"She must've been pretty confident the board would override Mr. Olson."

"She pushed hard in order to assert the freedom of the press," she said smugly.

"You don't think it was due to my article's quality?"

"Maybe. Partly. But more so for her academic rights. The article, after all, was a natural extension of ours on pornography."

"Really?" I didn't know if she was jealous or really believed it. (But I suppose she is partly right.) "I prefer to think Mrs. Webster believed in—"

Just then Mrs. W. walked over. She had overheard us. She smiled slyly. "Both of you can believe what you will, but the point is that the paper will be distributed next Wednesday and it will include many good articles." She began to leave, but then returned. She leaned over my shoulder and softly commented, "I would only fight for an article that I thought would do some good."

Friday, Late: No practice tonight. Everyone needed a break, so Miss G. canceled practice. At Hillcrest Pizza, Mr. Richter was training in a new person so he gave me the night off. A few local parties were planned but I have had enough of them. Steve, Walter and I went to Rochester, walked around the mall, then drove around.

What a week.

Saturday: A wet snowstorm hit the state last night. It melted by mid-morning, but before it did, driving was treacherous. The thick, wet snow that comes now is worse than January's nastiest blizzard. Winter has to get in one last punch before spring can come at last.

Sunday: Walter made a point of asking me to come to Sunday school today. I went and am glad I did. He appreciated Steve and me sitting by him. He wanted to explain to everyone what had happened.

He faltered some, stuttered at times, got confused on his

chronology, but it was the best "speech" I ever heard. It took a lot of guts to explain his mistake in going to the party and caving into peer pressure and drinking.

He cleared his conscience and maybe helped others avoid his mistakes. (My mistakes too—but "by the grace of God . . . .")

While he talked, some of the other kids shifted uncomfortably in the folding chairs. Maybe they thought the same things I did: Walter was caught by circumstances. I had luckily escaped and made it home safely.

Maybe some believed his temptations were unusual. It would be nice to think so.

But the person who surprised me most was Mary Arnold. She first stared at the floor, then shifted sideways in her chair so her face was hidden, then wiped away tears, then broke down and left. Pastor Jim's wife followed her. I can only hope things turned out well.

Maybe she wasn't the hypocrite I'd thought. Maybe she was just caught in things she couldn't handle.

It teaches me not to make quick judgments.

I have much to learn.

Judging is easy. Helping means work.

Monday: Musical week! Article week!

I'm off to dress rehearsal. I'm going early and take Amy—I'll need plenty of time to set up the lights.

Prom is end of next week. I've been trying to ask Sarah, but every time I try to talk to her, either she's been with someone at school or her phone's been busy. I should have asked her long ago, but it's been so hectic, prom just crept up on me.

Tuesday: Not much time before work, then I have rehearsal. The play's looking great. Miss Gunderson bought some ellipsoidals that cast a nice, sharp light. Using color gels, I can create interesting mood lighting, especially on night scenes. I also put gels on some of the older fresnels (Miss G. told me they are called that because they were named after a French engineer during Napoleon's time.)

The most challenging scene for the lights is the thunder scene, but the most moving of all is the final scene. I use a blue wash from the fresnels and keep a soft amber ellipsoidal on the von Trapp family.

—Gotta run—

After rehearsal:

I called Sarah and asked her to the prom.

Long pause.

"I already said I'd go with Steve."

"Oh." I couldn't hide my disappointment.

"I waited awhile," she said quietly, "but I didn't hear from you—"

"That's okay," I replied glibly. "We'll probably all sit at the same table for the banquet."

"Sure."

"See you tomorrow."

"Sure."

Click.

What a fool I am.

Wednesday: Double-length paper today. I've been depressed all day. The article was anticlimactic. Everyone had heard so much about its controversial nature that they assumed it would be extremely sensational. I'm afraid the controversy was created only by Mr. Olson. Most students seemed to think the article would have all sorts of titillating stuff about sex, but that wasn't the point of the article. It was about attitudes, about the need to see others as feeling and worthwhile human beings, not as objects to satisfy ourselves. I can only hope that it'll cause some to think a little.

Also, several weeks had passed since I wrote it. Re-reading it, I thought my sentences seemed rather stilted, not at all as I remembered them. Maybe that's the way with all writing. I wish I could go back and re-write it.

This disappointment, coupled with Sarah going to the prom with Steve, well, needless to say, I've been a crab all day.

Thursday: Opening night was a hit. The entire cast pulled together. Melanie was superb. And I must admit that the lighting wasn't bad either. Amy did a really nice job—so much better than in dress rehearsal.

A few days ago Miss G. said to me that everyone does better in front of an audience. As usual, she was right.

Friday: Another late night and another strong performance—except for one mistake. Somehow Melanie got confused and switched into her abbey costume too early. She then had to switch back before she could come on.

During that time, everyone had to ad-lib on stage. Miss G. jumped out of her seat and ran over to me. I was already whispering frantically into the headsets for details. Miss G. was asking the same questions into my free ear: "What's going on?"

Finally Melanie did make her entrance, but before that happened, the captain had to ad-lib an exit, then ad-lib a new entrance.

The funniest thing was that after the play most of the audience didn't even know anything had gone wrong!

Afterward, while we cleaned up: another disappointment. I was thinking I could at least drive to the prom with Walter, but he told me proudly that he was taking Karen Olson.

"So she and I can become friends again," he explained.

Oh well, maybe I'll be the only senior who stays home.

Saturday: Another great performance.

Later, at the cast party (Mr. Monroe helped Miss G. again) I ended up sitting by Melanie while we watched the video tape of the play. Amy was sitting on the floor with the younger kids.

Melanie leaned against my shoulder and spoke softly: "I am sorry I was snotty about your article. It was really very good."

"Thanks."

"You have good insight," she continued. I tried to listen to her words but I was suddenly enraptured by her nearness, her friendliness. I couldn't help myself.

"You're someone who I've felt I can be myself with," she was saying. She slid even closer and whispered into my ear: "A friend who doesn't make demands. That's why I didn't want to go out with you. I didn't want to lose that special friendship."

All the old feelings were running through me again, feelings I thought I had killed and buried forever but were now returning with renewed force.

Was she giving me an opening?

"Sarah said she was going to the prom with Steve."

"Yes," I said slowly. I felt delirious, light-headed. Was I dreaming? My mouth was dry. "Who are you going with?"

"Oh," she said, sitting up straight, crossing her legs. "I haven't decided yet."

"Well, may I add my name to your list?"

She leaned toward me again, coyly. "You may."

Now, here I sit at almost one in the morning wondering whether or not she'll choose me. I tell myself I should know better, but I guess I don't. I tell myself that I shouldn't care, but I do.

Sunday: I missed church but everyone else went. When I woke up, it was already too late to even make it to the church service.

When the family came home from church, the front door opened quickly. Amy dashed to her room and slammed her door.

Mom and Dad were arguing again—or, as it turned out, Dad was just angry at the world. He was taking it out on Mom. He wouldn't let her get a word in, but just kept attacking her for anything and everything.

I stayed in the kitchen staring at the Sunday paper, not moving. I heard him complaining about the church service.

"That preacher—God this and God that," Dad ridiculed. "God will take care of you, God knows what's best for you—"

Mom tried to interject some soothing words. I wanted to say: Mom, don't bother. He doesn't want to think differently. He enjoys his anger.

"Just tell me this," he howled, "if God is so loving, why did he take our farm?"

"Some things we can't know," she said meekly.

"Too many things we can't know," Dad spat, jerking off his tie. "Too many." He threw his tie onto the sofa where it lay in a twisted heap.

So much for a relaxing Sunday.

Later: 6 p.m. I just called Melanie. Her mom answered, sounding tired again.

Melanie came to the phone. I officially asked her to the prom. A long pause, then: "Sure. I'll be in pink. What'll you wear?"

"Gray, I guess."

"Good. That'll be a good combination."

After I hung up, I think I floated out of the kitchen.

Monday: When I awoke this morning, Dad was already up, eating breakfast and reading some leftover part of Sunday's newspaper. Mom was fixing bacon and eggs.

"Morning," she called.

"Morning," I mumbled, half asleep, and I staggered into the bathroom.

When I came out, Dad was watching the morning news in the living room.

As she always had on the farm, Mom brought my breakfast over.

"I've been meaning to tell you that Grandpa said he appreciated your visits."

I grunted my thanks.

The adrenaline high of the play had now run its course. I sat at the table like a deflated balloon. I didn't feel like talking at all.

As I ate, Mom went to wake Amy.

Mom cheerfully re-entered the kitchen. "Everyone I talked to was really impressed with the musical."

Amy staggered into the kitchen, her hair a mess, and plopped down.

"How's our actress today?" Mom asked.

"Tired."

Dad stepped into the kitchen before heading to the bathroom to shave. "I was proud of you both," he stated rather gruffly. "The play was good." Then he was gone. He said nothing more about the production.

Mom beamed.

Amy and I exchanged shocked glances. A compliment!

After school we struck the set. My last play. After the flats were stored, the props put away, the stage swept, Miss G. turned out the lights. As the curtain closed on the stage for the last time, a part of my life ended.

Tuesday: After school I drove to Rochester and rented a tux. I know a lot of guys wear suits but I don't want to be just anyone, not with Melanie.

I was lucky the rental store would even consider my order this late.

I also ordered a corsage at the Main Street Floral. When I got home I waxed the car. Later in the evening I called Steve. He and Sarah are doubling with Walter and Karen—Walter can't drive. If I had been taking anyone other than Melanie, I would've offered to take Walter too.

Even if I try, I can't imagine taking Melanie to prom. It seems like Friday will never come.

Wednesday: Another scandal twisted by rumors and insinuations. The Superintendent (Mr. Olson wisely stayed out of it) was allegedly going to bar Walter from the prom because Walter had been drinking the night of the accident. By the end of the day, however, the Superintendent decided that police reports couldn't be used. Students could be declared ineligible for activities only when school officials caught them.

I'm happy for Walter. I wonder, though: a student must be pretty naive, like Amy, for any student ever to get "caught."

Thursday: I have now ordered graduation announcements. Mom and Dad want me to have an open house like everyone else in Hillcrest. I'd just as soon not have one. Open houses are such work for the parents. Others, including some parents, wonder who can put on the biggest spread.

Who's the open house for? Seniors or parents? Most of my friends will be at their own celebrations. The only people left who can come to mine are relatives and church members. Oh well, I guess it is part of the ritual.

Tomorrow is the big day.

Juniors and seniors have to be in school all day in order to go to the banquet-prom. For the first time all year, I bet the upper classes have perfect attendance.

Saturday: I shall try to record last night accurately, honestly—

I went to Melanie's at six p.m. I finally met her mom when she answered the door. Mrs. Johnson, with no speck of gray hair, is Melanie's height and has the same high cheekbones. Her makeup was a bit too thick and couldn't hide the wrinkles around her eyes. Nevertheless, she was attractive for a mother and no doubt the boys once flocked around her. (I remembered briefly what Grandpa had said about beauty.) Mrs. Johnson looked me up and down at least twice, finally letting me in, and, smiling, told me that Melanie wasn't quite ready.

I was extremely nervous. My stomach felt tied in knots. I sat on the sofa in the living room and snatched up a magazine just to have something in my hands, something to look at. After a few minutes that seemed forever I heard a rustle of fabric and glanced up. Melanie walked around the corner. My breath caught and I think I flushed. Her hair was all swirled up and she wore an elegant, ruffle-bottomed, pink dress that accentuated her slender waist and bare shoulders. It reminded me of someone from *Gone with the Wind*.

I was glad I had been able to rent a gray tux. My hands trembled as I handed her the corsage. She and her mother fixed it onto her wrist, and then she pinned on my flower.

Her mom snapped a picture of us, and Melanie whispered into my ear, "You look nice."

"You look great," I gushed.

I opened the door for her (almost closing the door on her dress!) and we drove to Rochester. I didn't speed. I was in no hurry to share her with the group. We talked mostly about small, unimportant things. I'm afraid I wasn't able to impress her with my conversational skills for I was too overwhelmed by her nearness, her beauty. I don't even recall driving up to the Holiday Inn. After dropping her off at the door, I parked the car.

As I hurried to join her, I mentally snapped a picture of her by the glass entry—her elegant pink dress and the sunset's matching pink glow behind the hotel. I didn't want that moment to end.

Entering the dining area, we found Steve and Company among the gathered students. We also talked briefly to the chaperones who included the Websters. The administration had nothing to fear from troublemakers: Mr. Webster made an extremely intimidating bouncer.

I spied Aaron and Jennifer on the other side of the crowded room with a group of her friends. I waved. He waved back. Jennifer was beginning to show her pregnancy; she looked a little plump in the face and thick in the waist. I was pleased to notice that Aaron seemed in one of his happier moods.

In fact, everyone appeared to be in excellent spirits. Last year's prom (I was told) had been ruined by several drunk seniors. One of them, after hastily introducing the program, dashed out into the parking lot where he proceeded to throw up. A chaperone followed, but the senior drove off, leaving his bewildered and angry date behind.

There were no signs of that happening this year. The meal was pretty good but not as good as I had expected. I guess hotel food never is.

The program that Bob S. and Cliff Sorenson wrote and presented was moderately funny. It was a class history, a compilation of crazy "remember-whens." In the middle of it, Melanie asked me if I had left the car unlocked.

"I guess so," I replied. I couldn't recall for sure.

"Good," she smiled, looking relieved.

I was going to ask her why, but Steve pulled on my sleeve. "Are you going to meet us later for a walk by Silver Lake?"

I hadn't thought about it nor had I discussed it with Melanie. "Maybe," I answered. I was still trying to remember if I had locked the car or not.

Following the program each couple was officially photographed. Melanie is so photogenic. As for me, I was a nervous wreck. The photographer had to take several shots because I kept blinking. After all the couples were finished, the photographer took a total senior class picture. I think everyone signed up for a copy.

The dance itself was disappointing. Dances are often mediocre, but this one was worse than usual. The class had selected a band over a sound-system. About half the students left early. I didn't want to leave, not because I enjoyed the band, but because I wanted the evening to last forever. Melanie, however, finally suggested that we go. As we departed, I passed the chaperones and wished them a good night.

When I got in the car (opening the door for Melanie first) she slid closer. "Shall we drive to the bluffs? Lisa brought us a gift."

On the floor of the backseat lay a paper bag. That was why Melanie had asked if the car was unlocked. I reached back and looked; inside was a bottle of hard liquor.

"Figures," I muttered. "Lisa."

Melanie stiffened. "What's wrong with Lisa?"

"Nothing," I stammered quickly. "It's just, well, it's a long story."

Melanie relaxed and seemed satisfied. I had planned on meeting the group by Silver Lake but the thought of being alone with Melanie on the bluffs—

It made my mouth dry, my feet cold.

I drove to the bluffs.

As I turned into the parking lot, we spied several other Hillcrest cars. I parked a little distance from the others.

Melanie hiked her dress up, spun, and knelt on the seat. My heart was racing faster than I thought humanly possible. She reached back and grabbed the bottle. She sat again, straightened her dress, and opened the bottle. "Like some?"

"Okay," I said hesitantly, not at all excited by the prospect. "Remember, I'm driving."

"Cautious Chad," she smiled. "But I'm glad you're that way. I just need a little to . . . to relax."

"Go ahead," I said, but she had already started. I felt nervous, uncomfortable. At least where I was parked on the edge of the bluff's parking lot, we'd see any police coming and could pitch the bottle.

I tried to make conversation. "Your mom seemed really nice."

"She's alright, some of the time." She ran her thumb over the bottle's side.

I put my arm behind her, slid closer. "Oh?"

"She drinks too much."

"Oh. Do you see much of your dad?"

"He's on the road quite a bit. Likes it that way." She took a second swig from the bottle. Soon her breath smelled as it had at homecoming. "He says there's more excitement on the road."

"Oh." Her shoulder was smooth, like a soft flower petal.

"What about your parents? Your dad seems friendly."

"He is. To others. He doesn't say much to us, at least not much that's friendly."

"At least you see him."

"I guess so."

"What about your mom?"

"She lets Dad get away with too much. She waits on him all the time, letting him say whatever he wants."

"I suppose everyone's bothered by their parents."

"I suppose."

She offered the bottle. I acted as if I took a big drink but only took a small sip. Conflicting thoughts and emotions battled within me. The excitement of doing something illegal and dangerous pumped through me. Yet I knew it was stupid. At the same time I didn't want to offend Melanie. And I desperately wanted to make this evening special.

Then, like a cold splash of water in my face, I remembered Walter's accident. I didn't want to blow this night as he had. I suddenly felt hot, realizing my hypocrisy, like looking in the mirror and seeing something I didn't want to see.

She shifted close to me, took another drink.

"Don't you think that's enough?" I said.

I shouldn't have said anything—she instantly flared up.

"I'll do what I please."

"Sorry."

"Oh, that's okay." She relaxed, leaned against my side. "That's what I like about you. A good friend, like a brother."

I turned to face her. "I don't want to be a brother," I stated. I quickly kissed her.

She hesitated at first. Her lips were tight for a moment or two, but then she responded with a soft and passionate kiss.

She finally pulled back and I smelled her strong acidic breath and she looked at me as if she'd forgotten herself—or me—for the moment. I wished she hadn't taken the drinks. I suppose I smelled the same now.

She playfully slapped my chin. "Not too fast," she said, drinking again. "I need to relax, unwind."

I had no idea she drank like that. I recalled her paper on alcoholism. Mom had once said that Mrs. Johnson drank a lot.

I briefly wondered if Melanie's mother was an alcoholic. A lot of things suddenly started to make sense, like pieces of a puzzle quickly fitting together.

But I didn't care at that point. I gently caressed her soft, bare shoulder. She snuggled closer, made a purring-like noise.

We kissed again. I forgot about the drinking, forgot about everything except the sensations of her lips. Then she pulled back.

"If I'd have known you were this quick—" she laughed.

"Quick?"

"A few of the girls got rooms at the motel," she giggled. "Should I have?"

"What for?"

"For . . . whatever." It wasn't a cold night but my feet were as numb as if I'd been standing barefoot in a snowdrift. I felt dizzy, as if I were teetering on a very high and slippery roof.

I kissed her again.

She responded like I couldn't believe. I slipped my left arm around her waist. She took my hand, slid it onto her breast. I began to pull away, but she held my hand there.

My pulse raced as wild thoughts and feelings and sensations rushed into my head.

After a while, she finally moved my hand away and whispered: "Would you like to go elsewhere, somewhere more secluded?"

I took a deep breath and regained what little composure I had left and thought she was trying to cool me down. I grinned, raised my eyebrows. "Maybe less secluded," I said, trying to sound both clever and gallant.

I thought she would've appreciated my attempt at being a gentleman.

She didn't.

"Whatever," she said curtly.

"What's wrong?"

She said nothing, just stared ahead.

"What are you mad about?"

"I'm not mad." She crossed her arms.

I was confused, uncertain. "I . . . I didn't want to get, you know, carried away."

"After I worked so hard to relax?"

I kept my arm around her but sat up straight, slid away a bit. "I don't get it," I said.

She looked directly at me, sternly, and bit her lower lip. Her blue eyes looked hard and angry and she was about to say something but suddenly she didn't and she glanced down. After a moment: "Maybe you wouldn't."

I slowly pulled my arm away. I waited.

She said nothing.

I slid closer to her. "Listen, I—"

She turned abruptly and stared out the window, across the dark bluff, across the lighted city below.

I sighed. She still said nothing.

I wanted to cry. Instead, I started the car.

I drove to Silver Lake, frustrated and upset. She sat, arms crossed, unaware that she was crushing her corsage.

When we arrived at Silver Lake, I saw Steve's car and several others I recognized. I saw no sign of anyone.

I parked my car. "I'm sorry," I sighed, resting my hands on the steering wheel. I didn't know what else to say.

She said nothing. We sat in silence.

"I guess I don't always know the right thing to do," I said.

Finally she sighed and broke her silence. "I'm the one who should be sorry. I've always picked my dates carefully. And I haven't gone out much, not with different guys, I mean. Jay and I got back together and he was going to take me to the prom, then two weeks ago we broke up again. He wanted, well, I'm not sure what he wanted."

I felt like a real loser. "So I'm a second choice."

She turned to me, regretting, I think, that she had said anything. "It's not that, Chad. You're a good friend. I feel safe with you and I don't have to put up walls or pretend to be someone I'm not. I knew you were interested in me a long time ago but I didn't want to lose that good friendship."

"Until you needed a date."

She studied my face, then touched my arm. "Maybe. I'm not sure. But after I read your article, I thought to myself, this guy really is different from other guys I've known."

I looked out at the lake, and the moon was reflected on the dark water. "How so?"

"You didn't hide the fact that you felt it wasn't right for guys to, well, use girls."

"That shouldn't have surprised you. We wrote that in our pornography article. Remember? Not seeing people as things?"

"I know, but I didn't really understand it then. Or I didn't want to understand it. Not the implications. After I read your article, I wanted to know if Jay loved me for myself . . . . so, I told Jay no. He threw a childish tantrum and said he didn't want to see me again."

She suddenly turned away and began to cry. "Then tonight, I got to thinking. It was prom night. I didn't want to, but I knew it was expected. Maybe not by you but by others, at least some others. So I tried to get myself up. And here I find out that you really aren't interested—" Her voice trailed off.

I put my arm around her. "I am interested. I've been interested for a long time, but I don't feel it's right. I've always been taught that sex comes after marriage." I looked across the dark lake. "I didn't fully realize until tonight how much I actually believed it."

She cried harder. "If I could go back," she said between sobs. "I'm no different than the girl in your article, the one called those names."

As for me, my mind was whirling again into confusion. If only Steve were here, I thought. He'd know what to say, how to comfort, how to fix this mess.

I tried. "You are different. You care about yourself. I wouldn't want to be with you if I didn't think you are special. I'm not the one to talk to, but I know that God can make a slate clean, that anyone can go back. Christ made it possible." I stumbled through some more phrases that I knew well, phrases that were only now beginning to make sense to me. If it had taken me so long to really understand God's love, how could I make that idea intelligible to her?

She cried some more. When she finally stopped, she wiped her eyes and we got out and walked awhile. I put my coat over her shoulders. By the path along the shore, we met Steve, Sarah, and the rest. In the dark, though, no one saw that Melanie had been crying. Or at least no one let on.

We got home about two in the morning. Steve and the rest were meeting at his home for some videos and an early breakfast.

Instead of joining them, I took Melanie home. We didn't talk about what had happened—or hadn't happened—again.

She gave me a friendly good night kiss and I drove home, crawled into my cool sheets, and slept until noon.

Saturday Afternoon: I desperately wanted to help Melanie last night. I didn't know the right answers but I do know where I can find them . . . .

Sunday: I talked to Mom Saturday night and Pastor Jim today. I asked him just a few questions and he buried me under a mound of verses.

"Look them up," he said. "Don't believe what I tell you. Believe what the Bible says."

I read that book—finally—that he had loaned me. The historical evidence for the resurrection is incredible and undeniable. Before this time, though, I would have said that I had an open mind, but I didn't really want to look at any evidence. I wanted to have God when I needed Him, but up until the time that I did need Him, I'd do as I pleased. I wanted God on my terms. In my time. Now I clearly see the war that was raging within me and the war that still rages within Melanie and Dad.

Like Melanie, I wish I could go back, wish I could do my senior year over. What things I shouldn't have done bother me and what things I could've done haunt me.

After supper I called Steve and asked him to pick up Walter and come over.

"You two have been with me through my struggles this year," I told them when they sat down in my room. "And you've been good examples." Walter looked down, embarrassed. "I mean it. I've not put Christ first in my life. I've been too proud and I've been too afraid, but I want to start doing that now. Will you help me? I need to be accountable to others."

Steve grinned. "What else are friends for? It seems to me that we can all help each other."

Monday: Schoolwork never lightens up. I have a presentation on the Lake Poets Wednesday, my yearbook section of the 125th anniversary is due Thursday, and we have a trig test on Friday.

I want to find time to finish reading a book Steve gave me on forgiveness. It talks about the need to forgive others. Even though Dad's never said he's sorry, I know I need to forgive him. I can't hold onto my anger. God gave us the example by reaching out to us first. God allows us, then, to let go.

Will I be able to talk to Melanie again about this? She said she wanted to start over.

I'm afraid to talk to her, afraid as I've never been before. I don't know what she thinks of me, not really. But maybe that is where faith comes in.

And I'm also confused about my feelings toward her. Knowing that she's been to bed with at least one of her past boyfriends has altered my feelings. Somehow, in some vague way, I feel differently about her. Am I insensitive? Prejudiced? Does that mean I'm unforgiving?

God lets people start over. Can't I do the same?

I have much to learn.

Tuesday: Miss G. had a general call for help with rearranging set pieces, flats, and lumber in the storage area above the stage wings. Most of the people who had been in plays helped: Steve, Cliff, Melanie, Walter, and others. The one student noticeably absent was Bob. No one seemed surprised. He never helped with the sets, as if that were beneath his dignity.

When we were moving stage flats, I had a brief chance to talk to Melanie. Hoisting up a flat, I asked her if she'd like to get together to talk about some things.

Grabbing the next flat, she glanced at me and cautiously agreed to get together sometime.

I had to dash off to Hillcrest Pizza before all the stage work was done, but I'm glad I was able to help Miss G. a little.

Before this year I never dreamt that I would've been in plays and enjoyed it. I looked back at the stage door as I left the building. It was hard leaving. Another chapter of my life was closing.

Work was busy. A lot of track, baseball and softball players came in after practice. The extra hours I worked were good, though, because I need to put in as much time as possible. When summer vacation starts, Mr. Richter will be cutting back on everyone's hours. During the summer Hillcrest Pizza just doesn't have the business.

I'm hoping to pick up some farm jobs. Mr. Leroy will probably hire me again. I think most of the seniors are now thinking seriously about stockpiling college money.

For the first time I'm really committing my future to the Lord. I'll go or work where He wants me too.

Surrendering to God's will. It's such a simple concept. Why did it seem so hard to do?

Wednesday: I should be hearing soon from the University. Mom and Dad completed the financial form a long time ago. I'm praying that if I should go there, the school will come up with some financial help.

Each day I've been reading more of the Bible. Correct that— I must be honest: I've been reading the Bible for the first time in my life, really reading it. I feel my mind is growing so fast. I wish my life would be improving at such a rate.

I called Sarah to see if she'd like to join me go-carting in Rochester along with my church's youth group.

She said she is already going—and Steve's picking her up.

I couldn't hide my disappointment, even over the phone.

"But I'll see you there, right?" She's always such an optimist.

Now I have to go with the group or it will look as if I'm staying away because she'll be with Steve. I'd just as soon stay home . . . for that very reason.

No more time to write. My part of the 125th edition needs finishing touches.

Thursday: The entire journalism class worked on laying out the 125th in one massive editorial session. I think Grandpa will be pretty proud to have his memories part of the booklet. He will also be surprised to see his wedding picture in it. I didn't tell him I got a copy from Dad.

After school I went to the track meet. Steve was in the 800 meter run and the long jump. Walter throws the shot put and helps manage. As he has the last two years, Steve will probably go to regions. Walter could possibly make it to state. Lately he's been lifting weights both before and after school.

Melanie was at the track meet for a short time. At first I hoped that she had seen me walking out to the track after school and followed, but that wasn't the situation. Hillcrest ran against Cherry Grove and West Concord. That meant that Jay ran against Steve.

She did, though, sit with me by the outer chain-link fence on the hill overlooking the track. We talked a bit. A slight breeze cooled the heat from the bright sun. She wore shorts that showed off her already-tanned legs and a loose pink blouse. The breeze lifted her hair. Feelings were swirling within me, and, like the wind, were impossible to catch, impossible to examine, impossible to hold.

I began to tell her of my new commitment to Christ but I'm afraid I beat around the bush. I did tell her that I was reading the

Bible and learning for myself what I had previously only been told. "Last night I was reading how the Apostle Paul's life was turned around. Because Jesus paid the penalty for us, we can start over—"

She cut in: "I have an aunt who is into religion. She's nice, but gets pushy at time." She scanned the track field. "Mom often gets mad at her."

The runners were finishing the 400, getting set for the 800.

"Melanie, I know we've had some twists in our friendship, but I'd like to start again." I leaned toward her, smiling: "Would you do me the honor of joining me on a go-cart expedition Saturday?"

She looked at me sideways and the wind swept several strands of hair over her eyes. She brushed her hair aside with a graceful flick of her wrist. She stared at me for a moment with her large blue eyes and partially returned my smile. "I've never gone go-carting before." She glanced down onto the track, and I thought she'd agree to go, but then: "Sounds fun, but I don't think so."

"Something else then?"

"I don't think so. Maybe you're right about God and starting over but you know too many things about me. You need someone else." She sighed, hugging her knees up to herself.

"I don't want to go out with someone else."

She looked up, closed her eyes, let the sun warm her face. "Yes, you do. Someone more . . . innocent maybe."

"I'm not—"

She interrupted me, putting her hand lightly on my arm but never looking at me. "I've thought some about prom night. Maybe deep down I wanted to see you give in, maybe then—" She didn't finish her sentence but faced the wind for a moment before looking directly at me. Tears rimmed her eyes. "Let's remember our good talks, our good arguments, our good editorials." She ran a hand through her hair and leaned back against the grassy hill. "They were the best, you know."

"I know," I said. "Mrs. Webster thinks they'll get a journalism award."

"But we won't be around next year to receive it."

"I suppose it won't matter, once we're in college."

"No. I suppose not."

The 800-meter run was starting. Steve set up in the outside lane. The gun went off. Melanie suddenly sat up and leaned near me and kissed my cheek and for the briefest moment I smelled her perfume. "I'm going closer to watch Jay. For old time's sake."

"Okay," I said. She ran gracefully down the hill. I slid back against the cold wire fence and watched her go.

Friday: I've completed all my schoolwork. I put in extra hours at Hillcrest Pizza but the money doesn't help.

I dreamt about Melanie. I woke up.

That's all there is.

Not even a page tonight. Good enough.

Saturday: A beautiful day. Warm sun, cool breeze. Tulips are up. I mowed the lawn.

Went go carting. Pizza (of all things) afterward. Steve and Sarah acted pretty chummy, holding hands on and off, and Walter had asked Karen along. I spent my time with some of the younger kids.

Steve tried to include me but that made me feel more than ever like an outsider. Inside I felt like crying. I've missed so much.

I lost Melanie.

Who am I kidding?

I never had her.

I might've been closer to Sarah but missed that.

I know it's not the end of the world. It shouldn't matter. I tell myself it doesn't. I tell myself that, but I don't believe it.

Maybe that's still my problem. I want to fit into a group, encircle myself with a solid wall of friends.

I'm afraid to be myself.

Me.

Alone.

But self-sufficient isolation isn't the answer either. I read last night in the Bible that God can and will supply all our needs. Maybe He's trying to teach me that He is all I need, that He is both my island and my bulwark, my friend and my helper. I'm going to find that verse again and memorize it. Maybe I should start memorizing many verses. Having been in plays, I now know that I can memorize.

Sunday: Grandpa died.

Monday: We're almost ready to leave for the visitation.

Grandpa never saw the anniversary booklet.

I'm glad now we had those talks, that I recorded them. The funeral is tomorrow. We shouldn't have been surprised. His heart was beating irregularly. The doctors said he died quickly. He never made it to the hospital. For some reason I thought he'd live forever.

But life is full of change.

I am glad that Grandpa didn't linger on and on, struggling to live in pain. I know that he was ready to leave us.

Mom told us that Grandpa never wanted any heroic measures. When it was time, it was time.

Mom brought his things home this morning. The nursing home staff had carefully packed his pictures. Grandpa doesn't need to look at pictures anymore. He's with Grandma again.

The visitation is going to be hard. I'm afraid I'll cry.

Wednesday: Late afternoon:

Funeral is over. A weight has lifted off my soul. When Grandpa died, I knew that he went to heaven, but the funeral reminded me of it, made that fact more real to me, and helped me put his death behind.

How do non-Christians face funerals? Do they recall fading

memories? They have no assurance for the dead, no assurance for themselves. They have nothing to look forward to, no friend waiting to receive them. How horrible it must be to die without Christ.

What is Dad's spiritual stand? Grandpa said Dad just quit attending church. All Dad ever does is complain. Does God still hold him in His hands? Or has Dad jumped out of his grasp? Is that even possible? God wouldn't choose someone and then let that person go.

I'd like to talk to Pastor Jim about Dad, but Dad might find out about it and his fury would be incredible. Mom might even get upset at me, thinking that I was criticizing Dad.

I know I should talk to Dad, yet whenever I do, my cheek begins to sting. I know that isn't right. I don't want it to be that way, but I'm powerless to change it.

Somehow I must forgive Dad for hitting me. I've been harboring this bitterness too long. The funny thing is, the longer I carry this resentment, the harder it is to let go. Once and for all I must forgive.

Like a funeral, I must put the body of bitterness behind me. Forgive.

Lord, help me. I am powerless to change it, but You're not.

I am writing this before bed:

Tonight I wanted to talk to Dad but he drove up to school this evening. I think he wanted to "work off" some of his frustrations.

The custodians are sprucing up the school for graduation and the 125th, so I'm sure his help was needed. When he came home, though, he was tired and crabby, complaining about messy kids, lax teachers, and foolish administrators.

I don't get it. It seems that when I want to walk the right path, roadblocks appear all over, more numerous than rocks in the spring.

Thursday: We had the senior recognition banquet tonight at church. After the catered meal, Pastor Jim "roasted" us seniors. He came up with some pretty good jokes and stories. He pulled out funny incidents from growing up that I had totally forgotten.

After the roast he complimented each one of us individually. He said he appreciated my unflinching honesty and inquiring mind.

That sure sounded good.

We were then put on the spot and had to say what we're going to do. I said I'd probably go into engineering at the University of Minnesota but I wasn't sure. I wanted some profession where I could work with my hands, see some concrete results, know that I was accomplishing something valuable. Then I thanked Mom for her prayers—they got me through my senior year. Then I said that whatever honesty I had I got from Dad.

Then I sat down.

Mom was blushing and Dad stared at the water glass in his hand. I hope they were happy, not embarrassed.

After the brief ceremony, parents took pictures and others congratulated us.

It's late now. No time to talk to Dad.

Friday: Big tests today. Do teachers decide to hit seniors with tests two week before graduation? They probably do, knowing that next week will be futile!

By the time I drove to work, my brain felt short-circuited from tests. And what a day to have to work—temps in the high 80's, low humidity, everyone driving around, a perfect summer day in May.

Maybe it was good, though, not to be outside. I could let my thoughts simmer down, my brain recharge. When I got home, Mom and Amy were washing dishes while Dad watched TV. The news was on.

"Wouldn't y'know?" he stated angrily. "Bumper crops expected! Analysts are predicting the best farm profits in years."

I knew he was going to launch into one of his bitter speeches again.

If I was ever going to say anything—

My mouth was as dry as cotton. I stammered: "Grandpa said, uh . . . ."

"Huh?"

"Grandpa said you've never forgiven yourself for losing the farm."

Dad stared at me, shocked. "When did he say that?" he snapped.

"When I visited him, about a month ago."

"He was wrong." He turned again to the TV. "God took it from me."

"Maybe God did," I said. My mind went blank. I couldn't say anything else. I looked down at my hands. I couldn't think what to say.

I turned away, frustrated, and went to my room. I sat at my desk, stared at the wall. Finally, I wrote a note to Dad. Here's a copy:

> Dad, you always told me to honestly speak my mind. It's hard to hear you always blame God. Maybe God did "take" the farm from you, but was God a partner on our farm? Did you ever commit the farm to Him? During all the years on the farm, I never heard you talk about God. Now, He gets all the blame. How is it fair to assign Him the blame now when He never got the credit before? These are my honest thoughts. I hope you don't hate me for writing them down.

I went downstairs, left the note on his pillow, and walked out into the night. I stood looking up at the stars, then drove around town, then out into the country. I parked on a dead-end county road near our old farmhouse, and I prayed.

When I came home about a half-hour later, Dad was still watching TV. I knew he'd be going to bed soon.

I went to bed first.

Saturday: A loud engine noise woke me up this morning. Before I was completely conscious, I thought we were back on the farm.

I sat up, remembered where I was.

I jumped out of bed, partially dressed, and dashed downstairs.

Dad had ripped a big patch of sod out of the backyard and was tilling it.

"I better go help," I said to Mom, buttoning my shirt on my way past.

"Eat something first," she said.

My farm training ran deep in me. When someone was working, you helped. No questions.

"Chad!" Her unusually stern voice stopped me at the back door. "Have some breakfast first. This is something he wants to do. It's not much, but it's farming."

"What made him decide to put in a garden?"

"I don't know. But he told me he was going to do it last night, right before I came to bed."

Extremely nervous, almost scared, I remembered my note. Was he putting in the garden because of it?

Still in the habit of making big breakfasts, she threw some bacon on the frying pan.

Later, when I went out to see if Dad wanted help, he said no. "You're gonna be away at school next year. I better get used to it."

"Oh."

He never mentioned my note. He wasn't angry or happy, just determined.

A robin landed nearby, eyeing the stray worms forced out of the soil.

I went back inside.

Dad hasn't said anything about the note. I suspect he never will.

Sunday: We all went to church. As seniors, Steve, Walter, Mary, and I sat in the fifth pew back. We were expected to sit together; in fact, we wanted to stick together one last time.

Our families were seated in front of us. The message was a particularly strong challenge from a visiting missionary. At the end of the sermon, the missionary asked us to bow our heads and pray. If we wanted special prayer, we should raise a hand.

After a moment's hesitation, I did. I looked up so that I could see if the missionary saw me.

Then I broke out in a massive sweat. Right in front of me was my father's raised hand.

I never said anything about it all day. I suspect I never will.

Monday: A great night tonight.

At the high school's award ceremony I not only received a journalism pin (which I expected) but Miss G. surprised me with the "Contribution to Theater" trophy. It has a dark walnut base, an engraved brass plaque, and attached gold drama masks. It sits in front of me even now.

I'll admit that I felt pretty proud walking up and receiving it.

Dad worked tonight and saw most of the ceremony. Mom and Amy came too. Amy even received a special junior high drama pin. Steve received the Hillcrest citizenship award. They also had the 125th booklets available. I picked up my free one and Mom and Dad bought several additional copies.

After the ceremony, group pictures were taken of the seniors who had been in plays, journalism, band, choir, and various athletic teams. I never knew people took so many pictures.

I wish Grandpa could've lived to see it.

I remember that when I was little I used to think that people in heaven could see us, but I don't believe that anymore. It would be too hard for them to watch us fumble through our mistakes. Watching us, they would want to cry, yet they couldn't. There are only tears of joy in heaven.

Tuesday: Toward the end of college prep today, Mrs. W. stuck her head in the door: "Miss Gunderson, are you still hiding your hands?"

Miss G. turned beat red behind her desk. The girls caught on first. She then raised her left hand and showed us her diamond ring. All the girls huddled around her while we guys sat back and talked about other things. It was great—with all the chatter, no time for an assignment.

It's funny, but even though I figured she and Mr. Monroe were dating, I never expected her to get married. Adults, I somehow figured, didn't change. But I guess they are always changing, as I am.

Wednesday: I never thought that these last few days of school would come! Now, however, they're going faster than any vacation ever did. The last issue of the *Gazette* came out today with my final article. Another ending.

The issue was a senior special. All our future plans were printed.

Soon our class will be scattered to the wind.

After work I drove past our old farm. I hadn't done it since we'd moved.

I headed south of town, down into the valley, up the first hill and turned right. Our place was just as I remembered it—the big white farmhouse on the hillside, the sagging barn still needing a coat of red paint, the long hog house only three years old.

The new owners weren't home. I almost drove up the lane, but instead I stopped the car and got out for a minute and stood by their new mailbox. I stared at the grove of hardwood trees for a long time. So many games I had played there. Standing there, I recalled one weekend when I was about nine years old. On that Friday night Dad had taken us all to a Rochester movie theater to see a western. The next day found me playing cowboy in the grove. Surrounded by trees, I built a fort made out of deadfall, then I climbed the tallest oak, only to fall and break my collarbone. Many memories were entwined with that grove, memories as thick as the vines and underbrush.

I stared at the new owner's name on the red mailbox. I touched the white letters of their name.

I got back in my car and drove down the gravel road to the pasture gate. It was unlocked. We had always kept it padlocked even when the cattle were in another pasture. When it was left open, couples would quickly discover the fact, drive up the hill, and make-out. The new owners would learn in time.

I swung the rusty gate open and drove Monty up the familiar hillside. I steered clear of all the bumps and rocks I had years ago memorized.

Stopping the car on the top, I stepped out. The sun was setting in a rosy line of clouds. From that spot, near the fence line, for as many summers as I could recall, I would sit in the evening, count the cattle, and study the farms lying on the flatlands due west. Sometimes the distant farms dotting the land toward the horizon would disappear into the evening mists hovering over the fields.

This evening the horizon was bright with the setting sun. In the clear air, the distant farms looked closer than they actually were.

Soon, the entire countryside would be dark.

The hill was a quiet, beautiful place.

I knew well what Dad had lost.

I wondered how many farmhouses would be there in five years, ten years, or if any would exist in twenty. The only farms that I could see surviving would be those bought out by giant corporations. Change was inevitable.

An east wind, heralding rain, was picking up, pushing at my back, gently rippling the grass. I took a deep breath, then exhaled, letting my breath mix with the wind.

I looked around one last time, then got into my car.

As seniors, we will soon be scattered to the wind.

But maybe, like seeds scattered, we'll grow, grow strong, stronger in a new soil.

Thursday: Last full school day. A few panicking seniors came in extra early and made up tests or missing assignments. Tomorrow will only be a half-day for seniors.

Our morning group was really subdued. I know we were all excited, anxious to move on, ready to move on, but I think all of us sensed that no matter what our intentions were, most high school friendships did not last.

Except for Aaron and Jennifer. They finally set the marriage date for late June. He asked me to be a groomsman.

I hope they'll have a good marriage. I pray that their baby will be a challenge that will pull them together and not drive them apart into solitary frustration. Aaron's working at a burger place in Cherry Grove. He'll probably be managing it in a few years. Jennifer doesn't have to make any career choices. Her choice was made months ago. Perhaps that's what she wanted all along. Freedom from decisions. Someone to love her.

Maybe her future will happen as she's planned.

Maybe.

But futures have a way of surprising us.

Friday: The last day of school is over. During graduation practice, Bob S. and several of the more extroverted clowns of the class did handsprings and cartwheels down the aisle.

Mr. Olson frowned and shook his head at their exhibition. I was surprised when he didn't get angry, but he probably sees this every year. After all, what's the use of shouting? What can he hold over our heads now?

After practice, most seniors drove around town, several taking spins in the school parking lot. "The seniors say they want to leave, but come back anyway," I could imagine Mr. Jameson saying as he shook his head at his classroom window.

I'm concluding this journal now: nine months of writing, nine months of memories, of questions, of growing up. My letter of acceptance came today from the University along with a financial package. At least I can see far enough to know where I'm going for the next year.

No more to write, really.

Sarah's having a party for the "gang" this evening. She's lined up an old Abbott and Costello movie, some Popeye cartoons, and lots of popcorn. Graduation is Sunday afternoon. My open house will run into the evening. After that, the summer begins and I'll work all I can.

Where the Lord is scattering me, I don't know.

I once thought that I wanted God to send a strong west wind that would carry me up a high, grassy hill where I'd be able to see a long way. But distances, like the future, can be deceiving. Seeing far isn't as necessary as I once thought. I have to trust the wind. And He who moves the wind.

# # #

~ The Beginning of *Passing Through Paradise,* the Second Novel in the *Ironwood County Chronicles* ~

"It looks the same, doesn't it, Angela?"

I didn't reply.

Standing beside the car, I stared at the new green metal town sign, population 424, freshly peppered with buckshot. Looking north into town, down the highway, I saw Paradise. Across the highway on our left were the athletic fields. Surrounding them were tall, full cornfields, almost ready for the first frost. It looked like any quiet town, but I knew better.

I shuddered. Some memories just don't go away, even after ten years. He drove north into town. Two blocks before Main Street he turned left, and we found ourselves passing the redbrick, three-story school, its windows boarded up. Graffiti was scratched in the metal doors. Pigeons fluttered around the bell steeple, its lightning rod askew. Weeds and tall grass covered the playground like a tattered, green shag carpet. Empty chains dangled from the rusted swing set. Several late-blooming, yellow-topped dandelions sprawled around the tirehouse.

He next drove past the house we had lived in. It was still an attractive turn-of-the-century two-story white house. The surrounding block, though seeming smaller, was just as quiet as I remembered it.

Daddy drove west past where Mrs. Oatley once lived and where Mrs. Turpin still did. Both women's names had changed over the course of time and though Sally wrote me what her mother's new name was, I couldn't recall it: she would always be Mrs. Turpin to me. Daddy next drove down Main Street, or what was left of it. Except for a combined convenience store and gas station on the highway, businesses had completely deserted Paradise. The empty Main Street buildings were boarded up, even the corner thrift shop which Miss Bloomsbury had owned. Of course I knew that she had relocated in Hillcrest a few years after we moved there, but I had assumed that someone would have taken over the business. The few brick buildings that weren't condemned had been converted into apartments.

As Daddy turned north onto the highway, I twisted in the seat, glancing back over my right shoulder. East of town stood the old depot—or what was left of it—a black scar of wood and a charred chimney reaching up imploringly to a blue sky. Several years ago Daddy told me that vandals had set it ablaze.

Vandals. I doubted it.

On the north edge of town we paused at the dilapidated rust-colored house on our right. The house still looked the same, still needing paint, and the lawn still looked the same, still needing to be mowed. We didn't have time to visit.

"I'll stop in on my way back," Daddy said.

Northeast of the rust-colored house stood Browner's Woods, dark green in the bright summer sun. The topmost yellow-tipped leaves of the gnarled oak trees rippled slightly.

"Ready to move on?" Daddy asked.

I nodded to Daddy and he drove north to my college orientation.

Before we knew it, Paradise was behind us, growing ever smaller in Daddy's rear view mirror, finally disappearing. Yet the year we spent at Paradise wouldn't disappear from my life so quickly. It never would. As we drove down the highway, Daddy didn't say anything and neither did I. At Paradise, our lives had changed irreversibly.

After my time in Paradise, I came to expect death at any

moment. "You got to have life to love life," Edgar Lee Masters wrote. I disagree. I think you've got to have death to love life.

It was in Paradise that I stumbled onto a corpse, met my new mother, and Daddy and I were almost murdered.